THE TRAUMA MACHINE

THE TRAUMA MACHINE

ADVANCE READER EDITION

BRENT G. SPALDING

Edited by
TIM GRAHL

STORY GRID PUBLISHING

LETTER FROM THE EDITOR

Dear Reader,

I'm so excited for you to read this book!

Brent has spent years developing his craft, and *The Trauma Machine* is the extraordinary result of that dedication.

This is an early review copy ahead of the official release on January 13, 2026. There may be a few typos or small corrections we'll get sorted by publication day, so please bear with us.

I would love to hear what you think once you read it. You can reach me directly at tim@storygrid.com.

Thank you for supporting new fiction and for being part of the Story Grid community.

Tim Grahl

CEO of Story Grid

Story Grid Publishing LLC

Nashville, TN.

Copyright © 2025 by Brent G. Spalding

Cover Design by Timothy Hsu

Edited by Tim Grahl

All Rights Reserved

First Story Grid Publishing Advance Reader Edition

October 2025

For my husband and best friend, Luis.
Miracles happen when you're around, my love.

Beware the Jabberwock, my son!

— LEWIS CARROLL

PROLOGUE

UNIVERSITY FACULTY REVIEW COMMITTEE TRANSCRIPT FOR TUESDAY, NOVEMBER 15

Faculty Review Committee President Dr. James Sullivan: Dr. Oyibo, on behalf of the committee, I thank you for appearing before us today. The committee has called...

Professor Navenka Oyibo: I did not realize this was voluntary.

Sullivan: Excuse me?

Oyibo: I was compelled to appear because I received an order to do so. You have no need to express gratitude as my actions were dictated by necessity, not volition.

[unintelligible murmurs from gallery]

Sullivan: [clears throat] Right. Okay. As I was

saying, the committee has called you here to discuss concerns over the treatise you wrote in collaboration with Dr. Margaret Mayfield. We have serious concerns that this treatise undermines the empirical foundation of our institution.

Oyibo: I did not claim we were speaking for the university.

Sullivan: No, but you have worked here for decades and have built a reputation beyond the students and staff. This treatise reflects on all of us.

Oyibo: Is that why I am here? Because you are concerned about our image?

Sullivan: You're a professor of philosophy...

Oyibo: I know that.

[soft laughter from gallery]

Sullivan: [unintelligible] And that comes with a need for credibility...

Oyibo: And metaphysics.

Sullivan: Excuse me?

Oyibo: I'm a professor of philosophy *and* metaphysics. My ideas are bound to be unusual at times.

[soft laughter from gallery]

Sullivan: Right. [shuffles paper] I'll cut to the chase, Dr. Oyibo. As you know, our funding situation is becoming very complicated with accusations that our university staff is promoting ideas outside the, shall we say, realm of acceptable parameters. Your recent work has gained some attention that we don't need...

Oyibo: I thought we were a university, Dr. Sullivan. That introducing ideas "outside the realm of acceptable parameters" was part of our mission.

Sullivan: Well, just the same, Dr. Oyibo, I must confess that this treatise contains a number of extraordinary claims, even for you. These are not peer reviewed...cannot even *be* peer reviewed. I don't see how they could be.

Oyibo: Dr. Sullivan, my theses have been unusual before. Why is this so different?

Sullivan: Dr. Oyibo, specifically it's these extraordinary claims around Dr. Mayfield's nephew...uh...[shuffles papers]

Committee Member Dr. Pamela Jenkins: Nathan Daniel Johnson.

Sullivan: Yes, Nate Johnson. And the events on October 17, in the year...

Oyibo: I trust Peggy Mayfield's testimony regarding the circumstances involving her nephew.

Sullivan: Well, Dr. Mayfield is not available for this committee to question in person...

Oyibo: Her journals are well-documented in the treatise.

Sullivan: Yes, of course. [shuffles papers] Uh, but

then, let me ask you about this device you write about... [shuffles papers]

Jenkins:[whispered] Dr. Oyibo writes here about the trauma machine.

Sullivan: Yes, that's it. Thank you, Dr. Jenkins. The device called the trauma machine. This device that you and Dr. Mayfield claim allowed her to...uh, Dr. Oyibo, where are you going?

Oyibo: You did not read the treatise.

Sullivan: Please sit down.

Oyibo: Ladies and gentlemen, with all due respect, I have work to do.

Sullivan: We're not done here.

Oyibo: You did not read the treatise that so disturbed your benefactors. How can I stand here accused if you cannot even be bothered understand the charges you make? Read the treatise, understand its terminology and intent, and perhaps I'll entertain a summons at a future date.

[light clapping from gallery]

Sullivan: Dr. Oyibo...uh, oh... [unintelligible] Well. [shuffles papers] Dr Jenkins, there anything else on our agenda today?

1

The uptown clock tower bonged the quarter hour as the weathered terracotta tiles of Luigi's Linguini appeared in the distance, nestled among a canopy of ember and rust maple trees. Nate Johnson, on foot, wouldn't get to the restaurant for another five minutes, making him twenty minutes late for lunch.

"Stupid, Nate, stupid, stupid," he chided to himself as he picked up the pace, reviewing his morning of misjudgments that prevented a timely appearance. He had overslept and then lain in bed for another half hour, pushing the thoughts out of his head. Finally pulling himself out of the covers at ten past ten, he made the bed especially neat to help keep his mind from wandering to thoughts of this day's dreaded anniversary. Washing the dishes helped as well, which is what he was doing when he heard a harsh chiming near his apartment's front door. His mother's antique bell jar clock scolded it was already eleven thirty.

Nate realized then he would never meet his sister on time. Calling her was out of the question, for she would already have been on the road from her job cashiering at the Fresh Mart. Having no car (or license to drive one) nor the funds for a ride share, he walked to the restaurant, hoping the shortcut along the old tracks of the Centennial Pacific Railway would shorten his path, but the route still took him over half an hour.

He approached the restaurant's glass doors. He imagined his sister's glare, reminding him again how, with him at twenty-six and four years her senior, she had still ended up the more mature sibling, the big sister to her older brother. His face burned at the idea. Cheryl would be annoyed having to wait, but by now she should know his habits well enough. It's her fault if she expected anything different.

He entered the dark restaurant, blinking as his eyes adjusted. Cheryl sat at a table near the entrance, a man standing next to her with one hand on a chair. For a moment, Nate was certain it was their father joining them after years of ignoring the day. He winced at the rising sting in his gut, considering whether he should turn and leave, but it was too late. Cheryl saw him and waved. As Nate's eyes adjusted to the dimness, he discovered with relief it wasn't their father but the owner Luigi, hunched and balding, chatting up his sister. The relief faded to apprehension as Nate approached the three empty seats around the table. He took the seat across from Cheryl where a glass of ice water was set.

"I'm so sorry to hear about your loss," Luigi said, pulling out the chair for Nate.

Nate nodded, unable to think of a response, and sat down. Cheryl didn't look at him, her eyes on Luigi as he rattled off the day's specials. The owner set the wine list in front of Nate as he spoke, and Cheryl reached over and snatched it away, placing it on her lap.

"I already know what I want to order," she said after Luigi finished talking. "I'll have the fettuccine alfredo."

Nate knew Cheryl didn't prefer the white sauces, but that this was what Aunt Peggy ordered every time they came here.

Luigi turned to Nate. "And you, sir?"

Nate glanced at the menu, feeling Cheryl's eyes glaring at him. "Same here, only with shrimp."

Luigi smiled and bowed, taking their menus.

Cheryl handed him the wine list before he turned and ran off to the kitchen.

Cheryl picked her phone off the table, looked at its screen, and then stared back at Nate, her eyebrows raised.

"I know I'm late," Nate said.

She lowered her eyebrows and leaned in, her eyes narrowed as she examined his face and inhaled through her nose.

"It's not *that*," Nate said, immediately regretting the sharpness in his voice.

Cheryl flinched and sat back. "Sheesh, I didn't say anything." She turned to fumble inside her beige tote bag that hung over the back of the chair.

Nate gulped from his glass of water, thirsty from his walk, and hoped the cool liquid might relieve the knot in his gut. He hadn't eaten all day and now he felt a queasy nausea setting in. The empty chair to his right, between him and his sister, felt like a dark abyss waiting to swallow him.

This was their first October 17 without Aunt Peggy. The annual lunch at Luigi's Linguini had been her idea ten years earlier, a time to gather in memory of Nate and Cheryl's mother, Kathy, at a restaurant she favored. Their father Dan stopped joining after the first couple of years, leaving it a tradition for Peggy and her sister's two children to keep. His best friend, Rico, had even joined them the past couple of years. He had lost his mother, too, on that awful morning and would always carry his scars. But since Rico and Cheryl's attempt at dating had gone sour, he seemed to have all but vanished from their lives.

Cheryl pulled a flat object out of her purse bundled in a red and gold scarf. She set it on the table next to her plate. Nate eyed the package but kept silent. Her eyes were downcast, and she seemed far away. He picked up his water again and drank, ice cubes flowing into his mouth. A group dining at the table next to him were sipping from glasses of wine and frosted mugs of beer. His tongue felt dry, his throat parched. He crunched his ice and swallowed, the sharp cold helping to ease his longing for more.

Cheryl's voice broke the thought. "Why *are* you late?"

Nate looked over at his younger sister. He ran his tongue, still numb from the ice, over his teeth, thinking of a response. *Dishes. The bed.* What had seemed essential to get him through the morning suddenly felt vastly unimportant. "I lost track of time, I guess. You know me."

"Yeah," she said, her fingers on the scarf wrapping the object. "I just thought, you know, *today*, I mean, *this* today, after…" She glanced at the empty chair between them, her eyes glistening, before settling her gaze back on her brother. "You *knew* I'd be alone here waiting. Wondering if you'd even show up."

Nate felt a sharp twinge in his chest, like a hot needle moving toward his throat. It was only *twenty minutes*, for god's sake. It was her idea to keep the tradition going this year. He'd rather have spent the day alone. If she insisted on always keeping him in line, maybe she could try harder for *him* today.

To Nate's relief, before he could turn his thoughts to words, Luigi arrived with their plates of hot fettuccine, setting each down in front of them. The aroma tugged at Nate's stomach.

Cheryl's face turned all smiles to Luigi, thanking him. Nate felt annoyance at the cheery performance he knew would fade once they were left alone again. Luigi bowed, wished them both to enjoy their meals, and then left.

They both turned their attention to their meals, and Nate poked at the pink shrimp with his fork before placing one in his mouth. The creamy flavor of the sauce opened up his stomach, and he realized just how hungry he was. He began spinning his fork in the pasta and picked up a large bite.

Cheryl looked at him, her plate untouched. "Did you notice that, maybe, I'm upset?"

Nate set his forkful of food down. "Jesus, it was just *twenty minutes.*"

She shook her head. "It isn't always about you, you know." She tapped the scarf-wrapped thing against the white tablecloth. "I've been carrying this around since last week, trying to make sense of it, and you know what? I can't." She unwrapped the object from the scarf and pulled out a black, leather-bound book.

Nate recognized it right away. It was their aunt's journal.

Cheryl held the journal in her hands, several yellow sticky notes jutting out from between the pages. "I thought reading this would help me understand what happened to her," she said, looking down at its cover. "But instead, it just made it worse."

His sister frowned, fighting back more tears. Nate shifted in his seat. "What…" His voice caught, and he cleared his throat. "What does it say?"

"I can't just tell you, Nate. It's too…it just makes no sense." Her face scrunched up again and tears ran down her reddened cheeks. "She really did go crazy, Nate. Worse than we thought. That last week she… she totally lost her mind." She put the journal down and picked up her napkin, burying her face. "Of all the people in the world, I never thought that *she*..."

His sister couldn't finish, but Nate knew what she meant. Their father was a hopeless drunk, with Nate following close behind his father's staggering footsteps. But Peggy had always been a rock. For the past eighteen years, since he was eight and Cheryl was four, their aunt had kept the family together after their mother's unsettling death. For the past ten years, Aunt Peggy treated Nate and Cheryl to their mother's favorite restaurant, sharing stories and fond memories of the woman they never got to know.

Cheryl blew her nose and looked up at Nate with reddened eyes. "You know, I always had Aunt Peggy to go to when I was upset. You and Dad always have me, but I only had *her*. And now...with her gone..." Cheryl handed the book over the table. "Nate, I need you to do something for me. I need you to read this." She held the journal toward him.

Nate stared at the leather-bound journal, keeping his hands in his lap. "Now?"

"No, read it when you get home. Just take it."

Whatever it was, their aunt's last written words had seriously distressed his normally even-headed sister. He stared at the book like it was a glowing-red poker and shook his head. "I don't want to mess it up."

Cheryl sighed and shook the book in her hand. "It doesn't matter, as long as you read it. I don't want it anymore." When Nate didn't budge, she added, "I marked pages where she wrote things about *you*, things you need to read."

Her eyes watered again and Nate, wanting to prevent another bout of sobbing, took the journal from her hand. He placed it on the table next to his plate.

"Promise you will read it?" Cheryl's pooling eyes were wide and stern.

"Sure, I promise," Nate said, wanting to end the conversation.

"Thank you," she said evenly and then looked down at her plate of food. "I can't eat." She dabbed her eyes and then folded the napkin, placing it next to her plate. "Let's just get it to go. I'll drive you to your apartment."

2

The two sat mostly in silence for the five minutes it took to drive Nate home. Cheryl commented about how warm it was for October, and Nate agreed. He didn't even need to wear a sweater. Though quiet and low-key, Nate still felt relief sweep over him as Cheryl pulled into the parking lot of Westcourt Apartments.

"Thanks." Nate exited the car with a brief wave.

"Call me when you've read it," Cheryl said, nodding toward the journal he gripped in his hand. "I want to talk about it."

Nate nodded and waved again, shutting the door. He turned to his building, a single-story L-shaped structure connecting four studio units by a breezeway on the south end of the complex.

Standing in front of the door to apartment 8, he held the journal under one arm while he fumbled in his pockets for his keys. He remembered his lunch. *Shit.* He left it in the back seat of Cheryl's car. Spinning around, he watched her car disappear onto Jefferson Avenue. He kicked his door in frustration.

"Stupid, Nate, stupid, stupid," he whispered as he pulled out his key and unlocked the door. He was hungry and was looking forward to eating his meal in the quiet solitude of home.

He stepped inside his apartment and froze. His frameless bed was disturbed, the sheets he left in firm tidiness now wrinkled with something flat on top glinting in the light. His eyes scanned the room, finding another disturbance: books scattered on the floor at the base of his bookshelf of cement bricks and wood planks next to his desk.

A thump behind the closed door of his bathroom stole his attention. Fury burned in his gut as he realized his home had been invaded. He set the journal on the floor, exchanging it for a baseball bat he kept by the bed.

"I've got a gun," he shouted, a lie since Cheryl had taken his away months ago, fearful he would use it on himself.

He stepped toward the closed door, listening and

gripping the wooden bat. He heard a scuffle behind the door, and he grabbed the knob and turned it. Surprised it was unlocked, Nate swung the door open in time to see the legs of someone scrambling out the narrow window above the bathtub.

He rushed to grab a foot but tripped over the bathtub edge and stumbled into the basin. The bat fell from his hands with a clatter. A thump vibrated the tiled wall as the intruder hit the ground on the other side. Nate scrambled to stand up, grabbing the bat again and lifting himself from the window's lower edge to peer outside just in time to see the intruder's shadow rounding the corner of the building.

He threw the bat out the window and then scrambled himself through the narrow opening, lowering himself down on the other side. On the ground, his feet bumped into the framed iron bars that should have protected the window. He kicked the bars away before picking up the bat and running toward where the intruder had fled.

The footsteps were easy to see in the late afternoon light, imprinted in the soft dirt that surrounded the back of the building. He followed them around the building, where they vanished at the edge of the sidewalk. Glancing about, he listened for any sound that might indicate where his intruder had gone, but he only heard his own deep breaths from running. After a minute, he followed the sidewalk back to the breezeway of his building and to his open front door.

"*Bitch*," he hissed to himself. The burglar could have returned and taken everything while he stood stupidly out in the back. It would serve him right for not closing and locking the door when he first stepped inside.

His room was quiet and, as far as he could see, not disturbed any further. He glanced at his desk, relieved to see the six laptops he was refurbishing for sale on eBay still stacked in a neat pile. His mother's treasured bell jar mantel clock, a gift from Aunt Peggy when he moved out of his father's house a year earlier, stood undisturbed.

He walked through the kitchen and then checked his closet. Nothing else seemed missing or disturbed. He went outside, shutting his door and locking the deadbolt, and then walked to the back and picked up the black bars from the dirt below his window.

The holes around the window where the bolts had been secured were mostly intact, so he placed the bars back into the slots, even though they were far from secure. The would-be thief had probably wrestled them off without too much trouble from the termite-eaten wood and gained easy entrance. For now, the bars were literally window-dressing.

Courtesy of McVey Land and Living, Nate thought. He would have to call his building's management to have it repaired properly. If experience was a guide, it would be a long time before that happened. Perhaps he could get Rico to put on some pressure. In the meantime, he would need to find a safe place for the few things of value in his unit.

Nate returned to his apartment. On the bed lay the object he first saw when he got home, a framed photograph that had been on the shelves above his books. Grunting, he bent over and picked up the journal from the coffee-stained carpet, his back beginning to ache from his recent escapade. He set the journal on the bed next to the frame and then stretched, rubbing his lower back. His stomach growled, reminding him he hadn't eaten at all today.

The room dimmed from the waning light outside, so he turned on the rusted rodeo floor lamp near the desk. Grabbing some crackers, he chewed on a few as he kneeled down and began picking up the seventeen trade paperbacks scattered on the floor. He glanced at a few titles—*Cloud Atlas, Slaughterhouse-Five, Time and Again, Twenty-Four Hours a Day* —as he chewed, swallowed some more crackers, and then placed the books in alphabetical order on the shelf. Once he was satisfied they aligned neatly, he turned toward the bed.

The framed photograph that lay there was of Aunt Peggy, Cheryl, and him at the state fair a few years ago. He sat on the edge of the bed and picked it up, brushing away some accumulated dust. *"Pei-Pei,"* he whispered to the joyful face of their aunt, her arms around each of them, her long, white hair blowing in a breeze. The nickname was a private term of affection between him and his aunt, from when he was a preschooler and couldn't quite pronounce "Peggy."

He checked that a note she had written to him was still taped to the back and then set the photo on the shelf where it belonged. He returned to the bed and picked up the journal. Opening the dark leather binding to the first page, he read the scripted letters, *The Journal of Margaret Lynn Mayfield*. He flipped through some pages, passing through scribbled recipes and dated entries with brief paragraphs of events from the day. *Grocery shopping today, I forgot the eggs...Dan to AA Thursday at six, I can't let him skip again after last weekend...Cheryl is nervous about the new school. I tried to give her something to look forward to, maybe we'll have girls' night after the first week... Talked to Nate about his C in algebra. I know and he knows he can do better...*

Nothing unusual there. Nate fingered the edge of a sticky note pressed between the pages halfway through the journal, hesitating a moment. *I'll read just a bit,* he thought, *just to see what Cheryl was carrying on about.* He opened the journal to the first place that Cheryl had marked.

3

The Journal of Margaret Lynn Mayfield

...I remember the moment of impact, being thrown against the seat in front of me, the crunch of metal, the grunting cries of Katherine and Lois, the shout from Patrick, and then his crying. I panicked when I saw the flames, not realizing little Nate was crumpled on the floor, thrown halfway under the driver's seat. Fuel flowed over our car from the tanker we had just hit, flames licking outside the rear passenger door where I sat. I don't remember leaving the car, only finding myself outside and seeing my sister stuck in the front passenger seat, the shattered windshield like a glass blanket over her as she struggled to get out, the flames around the car growing.

I watched a group of men rescue her. They pulled the door open and yanked her out. She bled from cuts of glass and suffered just minor burns, but she was safe. The flames exploded into an inferno, engulfing the car, and Katherine shrieked.

"Nate!" she cried out. "Where's Nate?"

She turned to the burning car on her skinned knees, wailing as it burned before us. Lois and Patrick joined us, and we pulled Katherine away from the growing heat. She turned, her eyes boring into me as she struggled to take a breath. Katherine knew I had left her child behind, and she would never forgive me. My young nephew died in an agony of flame and smoke.

Yet I also have another memory. I know it to be new, but it originates from that same terrible morning eighteen years ago. It is what really happened. Or, more accurately, what really happened now.

We still hit the tanker. I still panicked and scrambled out of the car. But as I stood a safe distance from the scene, a woman in a green running suit emerged from the small crowd of bystanders and pulled Nate out from the other side of the burning car. I could see Patrick trying to follow them, but the flames blocked his way out and, to my horror, his clothes caught fire.

My memories become muddled at this point, perhaps blocked by the terrible inferno I witnessed. All I am certain of is that this is a new *memory. For I know still that Nate was the only casualty of that terrible accident, dead due to my cowardly negligence. I know, too, that Katherine and Lois died, Patrick got severely burned, and*

Nate survived unscathed by the actions of the woman who pulled him from the car. Both memories exist in my mind, each one vivid and true.

I remember both because I was that other woman who pulled Nate out of the burning car...

4

Nate pulled his eyes away from the words on the page. He stared at the journal, comprehension of the words he read triggering a deep melancholy. That car accident, eighteen years ago on this very day, remained the worst memory of his life. Aunt Peggy's bizarre double recollection seemed to show what Cheryl had claimed at lunch.

A sharp knocking at the door pulled Nate from his thoughts. "Just a sec," he called out, standing and walking toward the door. Peeking through the curtain, he saw a tall figure outside, a gray and blue shadow in the deep twilight. Nate recognized the curly hair and slight slouch. Rico.

Nate stepped back from the window and closed the journal. He scanned the room, looking for a safe place to store it, somewhere out of sight to prevent any prying questions from his friend. He carefully placed it behind the line of books he had earlier replaced on the shelf.

A renewed volley of rapping erupted. "Okay, okay," he said, returning to the door and removing its chain before then turning the deadbolt and opening the door.

Patrick "Rico" McVey stood at the threshold with a crooked smile, a blue cooler slung over his left shoulder. "Jesus, what's up? Did I catch you whacking off?"

Nate stepped aside, catching a whiff of mint vape mingled with cannabis as Rico stepped inside. His friend's left eye was bruised and slightly swollen, probably after an argument with his father. Nate knew better than to comment on it. "In your wet dreams, asshole," he said, giving Rico a good-natured slug to his shoulder. "What's up?"

Rico set the blue cooler on Nate's bed near where it sagged in the middle and then unzipped its cover. "I tried calling you earlier to let you know I was coming over."

Nate felt his back pocket for his cell phone. Empty. He patted his other pockets, wondering if it had fallen out during his encounter with the burglar. "I misplaced my phone," he said sheepishly.

Rico shrugged. He pulled out a plastic jar of

peanut M&Ms and shook it, the colorful candies rattling like a snake. "It's M&M Day, buddy. Did you think I'd forget?" He twisted the lid with his right hand, the jar held against his blue and green plaid shirt with his left arm to keep it steady. His scarred left hand dangled a bit from the sleeve as Rico struggled to hold the cannister steady, the remaining stub of his useless pinky finger extending out. He grabbed some of the candies and threw them in his mouth.

He and Rico hadn't had an actual "M&M Day" commemoration since they were teens. Rico came up with the idea in junior high, at an age where morbid humor replaced tearful memories. On that first M&M Day, Rico recited with mock seriousness, *"For our dear Mother and Mom, who, by God Almighty, are done and gone,"* followed by ripping open and devouring a large bag of the candy.

Nate's stomach growled at the sweet aroma from the cannister. He grabbed a handful of brown, red, and green M&Ms, and his mouth watered at the sweet crunch as he bit into them. "I haven't had anything to eat all day," he mumbled as he chewed the candied chocolate and nuts.

"No Luigi's this year?" Rico took another handful of candy.

"Cheryl and I met," Nate said, wiping his mouth with the back of his hand.

Rico sighed. "Yep. Of course you did."

"Yeah, but it was a bit…weird without Aunt Peggy." He coughed as chocolate stuck in his throat. "Cheryl and I left without eating."

Rico sat on the edge of the bed and scratched his goatee, his wounded eye twitching as he crunched through another fistful of candy. "Yeah, I miss her, too." He handed the cannister to Nate. "Aunt Peggy, I mean. Not Cheryl."

Nate took the candy. "You're still pissed at her for breaking up with you." Nate shot him a sly smile. "Cheryl, I mean. Not Aunt Peggy."

Rico picked a green candy from his hand and, with a wild grin, threw it at Nate. "Asshole."

Nate laughed. It felt good bantering again with his friend. He and Rico had been strangers since Cheryl broke up with him six months earlier. On this day in particular, it felt good to know he could still smile. He tossed the candy into his mouth, chewed, and then swallowed too fast and began coughing.

Rico reached into the cooler and pulled out two cans of Samuel Adams Boston Lager. "Here," he said, handing one to Nate with his withered left hand. "To wash that down."

"Rico," Nate said, spitting candied chocolate. "I can't. I just got my red coin. Three whole months."

Rico held the blue can toward him, dew from ice in the cooler dripping down its side. Nate licked his lips and coughed again.

"Jesus Christ, dude, I haven't seen you in months and I'm not letting you choke to death on me." Rico popped the can, the crisp snap followed by a spray of mist. "It'll just be between us buddies. No one else is gonna know, okay? Half the members of those groups lie about revisiting old friends, anyway."

Nate's mouth watered at the fresh, cold smell. *Yeah, who's going to know? Just a sip or two. Just to wash this crap down.* He took the can from Rico, the cool metal soothing against his fingers. The sweet, malty aroma sent a chill down his spine. He sipped, swishing the foaming lager in his mouth. His mouth tingled as he washed down the chocolate and bits of candied nuts.

He took a larger sip. *Just to wash down what's left.* The golden-brown taste filled his mouth, the effervescent coolness slipping down his throat. Nate took a large gulp—*The last one, I promise...*—and relished in the sensations, his head beginning to swim as the abrasive world around him turned softer. He shifted at the edge of the bed, the cooler behind him clanking with ice and more cans.

"Just the one," Rico said, raising his can. "To Mother and Mom. Cheers."

Even after months of AA meetings and all the talks and speeches on how there is no such thing as *just the one*, Nate accepted the convenient delusion. He raised his can and clinked it against Rico's. "What the hell. To Mother and Mom." He drank the contents down.

He floated in red darkness, the ticking of the clock seeming to match his heartbeats. *...did you notice that, maybe, I'm upset... she totally lost her mind...* He pushed his sister's voice to the back of his mind, her concerns no longer mattered. *I was that other woman who pulled Nate out of the burning car...* No, push that away, too. No weirdness. No worries.

He heard a squeak of the box springs he lay next to on the floor and then the clatter of ice along with a zipping sound, Rico getting another drink. *Fine, have one more for the road, buddy,* Nate thought, not wanting to vocalize and disturb the first peace he had felt in months. *Thank you, man. Thank you.*

A pounding on the door caused a flash of lightning brilliance in his head. His eyes popped open before could think about it, the ceiling light above him blinding and sending crackling pain behind his forehead.

"What the..."

"Nate! Open the door. Nate!" More pounding.

Nate sat up on the floor, five empty cans rolling near his legs. "Cheryl."

"Seems so." Rico stared at the door from the edge of the bed, his swollen left eye glistening against reddish purple skin. He leaned forward, swinging a can of beer in his good hand like a pendulum. More pounding. "Better get that."

Nate staggered to the door and unlocked the dead bolt and chain. Cheryl pushed her way inside, looked him up and down, took in the cans on the floor, and then glanced at Rico. "What's *he* doing here?"

"What? He can't have his own friends over to his own place?" Rico stood up.

"You're not his friend," she said, her foot kicking an empty Samuel Adams. She stepped to the side of the door and pointed toward the parking lot. "Rico, please leave."

Rico sat back down on the edge of the bed. "Maybe *you* should leave."

Cheryl sighed and turned to Nate. "Please, get him out of here."

Nate stood with his hand still on the inner front door knob, wishing nothing more than to return to that nothingness he felt lying on the floor just moments ago. He turned to Rico.

Rico raised a hand, palm out, to Nate. "Really, buddy? You're going to keep letting her drive your life? Do you want her picking all your friends for you now?"

"Rico…" Nate started.

"Get some balls, man. Maybe she can pick them out for you." He sneered at Cheryl.

Cheryl pointed a finger at Rico. "A friend wouldn't have brought Nate, who, you know, is an *alcoholic*, this shit." She kicked some cans, which clattered against the box spring of the bed.

Nate felt a rush of warmth to his face, his fingers gripping the doorknob. "Cheryl, he's right. You should leave."

She looked at her older brother, her mouth agape, shaking her head. "No, I'm not leaving. Not unless you come with me."

"*I didn't invite you here!*" Nate raged. He let go of the door and pointed toward Cheryl's car. "Go!"

Cheryl stepped toward Nate, her face red and eyes pooling, her hand outstretched and hesitant, as if she were considering striking him. After a moment, her hands fell stiffly to her side. "You're drunk, Nate. I can't leave you with him."

Rico stood up quickly and loomed over Cheryl, his chest almost touching her face. "He said get the fuck out." His eyes were narrowed, his right hand balled into a fist.

Cheryl looked up at Rico, her face paling. Nate stepped forward, trying to wedge himself between the two, but Rico shoved Nate back toward the kitchen. Cheryl stepped forward to help keep Nate from falling backward, grabbing his arm until Rico blocked her and shoved her with both his hands. Hard.

Both her feet left the floor as she fell backward, her hands gripping the empty air. Her plunge ended as her head struck the glass dome of the clock beneath the window. She cried a brief, sharp gasp as the glass shattered under her head, the weight of her body knocking over the small table on which it had sat. Her head cracked as it met the table edge before thumping against the glass and smashed clockworks spreading across the matted beige carpet.

Nate froze. Cheryl's eyes stared wide toward the ceiling, her body shaking and her legs twitching. Blood pooled behind her head, mixing with the glass and metal on the carpet underneath her.

Nate could only remember the minutes that followed in flashes, like photographs randomly scattered on the floor. Fumbling around his desk, looking for his cell phone. Blood around Cheryl's head, mixing with glass and metal, shimmering like a gruesome halo. Her eyes looking up, unmoving. Her legs twitching. *A dream,* Nate thought. *This is a bad dream.*

Rico paced the floor near him, staring down at a cell phone he held in his right hand. For a hopeful moment Nate thought he would call 911, but instead Rico stuffed the phone into his back pocket and ran out the open front door.

"Rico!" The name slurred from Nate's mouth while his friend vanished into the darkness. He lost his balance, the floor underneath him seeming to move like a ship at sea. His hands grasped at his stack of refurbished laptops for support, knocking them with him to the floor. His stomach churning, he heard Rico's car tearing out of the parking lot. He stared down at the carpet, unable to look over where Cheryl lay.

Long minutes later, the wail of sirens approached. Nate glanced toward the open door where a small group of neighbors had gathered. No one came inside as they gawked at Cheryl in a growing pool of blood, their mouths agape. He wondered if one of them had called for help, but the small group scattered as the sirens reached the parking lot. Nate crawled over to his sister, her chest moving with short, quick breaths.

Minutes later. Or an hour? Nate sat on the uneven asphalt of the parking lot, blue-red lights dancing around him. The neighbors had dispersed and gone inside, an instinctive distrust whenever the police showed up. Some peered out of their thin curtains, keeping out of sight so as not to risk any trouble.

A cop, a stout woman with dark eyes, asked him questions he didn't hear. A tall man in a blue shirt flashed a penlight in his eyes. The glare hurt and Nate looked down at his hands, mottled reddish brown with blood. Had he cradled Cheryl's head as they waited for the approaching ambulance and police? He couldn't remember. Out of the squawks of police radios and voices, a question emerged. "Do you have someone we can call for you?"

Police stood behind yellow tape inside the door

of his apartment as white flashed behind the closed curtains.

"My sister," he said, watching the stretcher being lifted into the waiting ambulance, a paramedic holding an IV above the supine form on the bed as it was loaded inside.

"She's being taken to Saint Teresa's Hospital. It is closest here. Is there anyone else?"

Nate thought of his father and shook his head. "Can I go with her?"

She placed her hand softly on his shoulder. "Not in your condition. I'm sorry."

Nate watched the ambulance doors close and the vehicle drive away, sirens blaring. Another cop walked over. "He give a statement yet?"

"I'm working on it," she said, a sharp clip in her voice.

"Well, we gotta roll, Ramirez. Shooting in Centennial Park."

The cops in Nate's apartment ducked under the yellow tape and ran past them as they muttered into their radios on the way to their squad car.

The woman sighed and stood up. "We just leave this?"

"It's just another domestic squabble at West*whore*. Besides, I doubt he's going anywhere. Another shift might follow up."

She nodded and the other cop walked back to their squad car. Ramirez leaned over Nate and extended a hand. "Go back inside. Sleep it off, okay?"

Nate took her hand and groaned into a standing position.

The officer turned him toward his door and gave a gentle push to his back. "Go on, now. Sleep it off."

Nate's shoes crunched against the loose asphalt gravel. Yellow tape stretched over his open front door. He stopped, wondering if crossing the police line would give them an excuse to arrest him. He turned to see if they were watching him, but the cops were already getting in their car. Nate watched until they pulled out of the parking lot, their shrill siren wailing. Nate turned back to his open front door and tore the tape. He left it to flutter in a breeze as he walked inside and shut the door.

Nate glanced where the clock had once been placed, the broken pieces and blood-stained carpet greeting him instead. He felt like a knife had entered his gut.

Thinking he would be sick, Nate ran to the bathroom. He hovered over the sink, but the nausea faded. A glint of color caught his eye from the bathtub, his cell phone against the white fiberglass basin. *Stupid, Nate, stupid,* he thought, queasiness creeping back as he remembered his fruitless search around the desk while his sister bled. He picked it up, turning it to view the cracked screen. It was almost ten o'clock.

Nate walked over to his desk. He couldn't sleep or sit around while Cheryl lay injured at the hospital, her life dangling like the pendulum on a clock.

Not in your condition. The cop's words burned in his mind. Fuck that. His sister was alone, and he needed to be with her. He would hitch a ride if he had to.

He put the phone in his back pocket and grabbed his thin, worn wallet from a desk drawer. Outside, he locked the door and stepped into the parking lot. Cheryl's car sat angled over two spaces at the front of his unit, as if she had rushed to park, no doubt after seeing Rico's car. Glancing through the driver-side window, he saw her keys dangling from the club she had placed on the steering wheel, a sign of her hurry to confront Rico, and now a blessing. Nate took a deep breath and pulled on the door handle. To his relief, it opened. He had found his ride.

Any brief respite from the evening's agony faded when he sat down. On the dashboard sat his forgotten lunch. Another punch to his gut, Nate gripped the steering wheel until his hands hurt. *I should be dead,* he thought. Cheryl had only stopped by to bring him the food he had left in the back seat that afternoon. *I should be fucking dead.* He picked up the container and threw it out the window.

5

On the road, Nate kept a firm handle on the steering wheel, his eyes glancing about for any signs of the police. He had surrendered his license to drive over a year earlier in court, but he intended to be a model driver, keeping his eye on his speed and resisting the temptation to rush his way to the hospital. Although discarded, the aroma of his forgotten lunch haunted him all the way. He parked near the visitor entrance and hastily exited, the automated glass doors swinging open as he entered the lobby.

A burst of cold air from the climate-controlled lobby brushed his face as he walked inside. He wore only a thin gray T-shirt and felt the hairs on his arms prickle as he walked with a slight waver toward the receptionist desk. Small groups of people sat along the walls on beige-cushioned chairs while a couple of young children played with plastic dinosaurs on the carpet before a glum looking middle-aged man. Behind them stood a mural of Saint Teresa of Ávila, the nun in prayer as a dove approached with wings spread, presenting a scroll in what appeared to be Latin text.

The young woman in a blue uniform smiled as he approached her desk. "My sister was brought here. Cheryl Johnson?" His voice cracked as he spoke and he cleared his throat.

"She's currently in surgery." The woman didn't look at her computer, and Nate wondered how she knew. Her next statement answered his unspoken question. "The gentleman around the corner is waiting for her, too." She leaned forward and pointed in the direction near a rack of cards, and Nate thanked her as he turned from the desk.

On the other side of the card rack sat a man in late fifties, leaning forward in his chair, his elbows on his knees and his face bowed down toward the floor. His eyes appeared closed.

The calmness of his father sent a burn of fury through Nate's chest. "What are you doing here, Dad?"

Dan Johnson looked up, his eyes bloodshot and his face pale. He looked at Nate as if he didn't comprehend him and then sighed as he sat back in the chair. "Cheryl's been hurt."

"I know. What are you doing here?"

"The police called me on her phone." Then seeing Nate staring at him, added, "I'm her father."

Nate looked away and kicked at the orange-and-brown striped carpet. "Some father."

Dan's eyes didn't leave Nate as he spoke in a clipped, even voice. "The last thing I need right now is your horse shit."

Nate flinched and crossed his arms. As he considered a response, a doctor emerged from a set of steel double doors and approached them.

"I'm Doctor Tanner, are you the father of Cheryl Johnson?" Lines creased his dark skin and his eyes had dark circles underneath.

Dan stood up and nodded. "How is she?"

"Cheryl's surgery was successful and we evacuated the hematoma to relieve intracranial pressure caused by the swelling."

Nate shifted on his feet. "Wait, swelling?"

"Cerebral swelling, from the head injury she sustained. That's the good news. Unfortunately, she also experienced considerable hypoperfusion… from the blood loss… which resulted in oxygen deprivation to her brain."

Dan stepped toward Nate and gripped his

shoulder for support. "Will she... will my girl be okay?"

Nate felt his father's fingers burn through his T-shirt but resisted the temptation to step away. He kept his eyes fixed on the doctor, who slowly tilted his head as he read a chart attached to a metal clipboard.

"Her vital signs are stable, and she is out of any immediate danger." Dr. Tanner's eyes shifted between Dan and Nate. "However, the prognosis for functional neurological recovery remains extremely guarded."

"What does that mean?" Nate stepped away from his father, a sharp pain growing behind his eyes. Dan released his grip and staggered back. The doctor helped him sit down on the lobby chair.

"It means it is unlikely... not impossible, but highly improbable... that she will regain a level of independence in her daily activities. Perhaps with dedicated rehabilitative therapies, her chances of some level of recovery are possible."

He then rattled off a series of therapies for movement and speech that glided past Nate. He thought of his futile search for a cell phone while Rico ran off instead of calling an ambulance, all while Cheryl lay helpless and bleeding to death. He gritted his teeth and shook his head. "Can I see her?"

"She's in recovery," the doctor said. "It will be a while before we can allow visitors, and a lot depends on her condition in a few hours. We will keep you informed, but there is no need for you to remain here." He ruffled though some papers on his clipboard. "Let's see, I have contact information…" and Tanner read off Dan's phone number.

"That's correct," Dan said.

The doctor nodded and excused himself, disappearing behind the chrome doors.

"I'll stay," Nate said, standing next to where his father sat. "You can go home."

"You can stay if you want, but I'm not leaving."

Nate paced in front of his father. "I don't want you here, Dad. I'm the closest to her. I'll stay."

Dan looked up, weariness in his eyes. "You don't get to decide that for me, Nate. I'm staying."

Nate shook his throbbing head. He couldn't go back to his apartment. He couldn't remain in the lobby with his father. "You're just waiting for when it is safe to clear everything out of her old bedroom," he growled. "Get that game room you always wanted."

Dan's face reddened as his back stiffened, his voice dropping low and harsh. "How did this happen, Nate? How did my little girl get hurt?" The chair creaked with sharp pops as he leaned forward.

"I know she was with you today. What happened to that big brother who used to look after her?"

Nate winced and turned to the card rack. *Wishing you a speedy recovery... With our deepest sympathy... Time heals all wounds...* He resisted an urge to knock the entire rack over. Across the lobby, the man with two young sons was sobbing, holding the children close while a woman in a white lab coat stood near, probably giving them the worst news of their lives.

Without another word to his father, Nate rushed out of the lobby through the glass double doors.

Heading to the car, Nate slowed his pace, wondering where he would go. He reached the car, unlocked the door, and sat down. The prospect of returning to the apartment felt like swallowing glass. He tapped his fingers against the steering wheel, his breaths sharp as he considered what to do. *What the hell*, he thought. He'd already lost his red coin. He started the car and backed out of the parking space. *I need to visit old friends.*

6

"Wake up."

"Wha... hmm..." Nate stirred on the bed, flat on his stomach. He kept his eyes closed and ignored the voice. His binge at The Stray Cat still hung in his mouth, a bittersweet edge of spice and citrus from the bartender's own special cocktails. His head swam through thoughts... the bartender got him a cab, he would owe him... oh, the car... need to pick up Cheryl's car at the bar... Cheryl... *Cheryl*... No, no more thoughts... best to sleep... let it go... moving on... nothing to see here...

"*Get up!*" A harsh voice hot in his ear. Fingers tight on his shoulder, shaking him.

Nate opened his eyes, the light hurting his head. He closed them again. "Sheeping..."

"No, get up." Hands firmly gripping Nate's

shoulder pulled him to a sitting position. Nate shook his head, dizziness coming over him. A pair of hands grabbed at his ankles and pulled his legs to the side of the bed so his feet fell to the floor.

Nate leaned forward, nausea blooming in his gut. "Oh, sick, sick…"

Hands under his arms pulled him to a standing position and half-dragged, half-walked him to the bathroom. "Get it out of your system. We have work to do."

Nate stumbled and fell on his knees at the rim of the bathtub. He inhaled deeply, trying to quell the nausea.

Hands shook him by the shoulders. "No, get this out. I need your head clear."

Nate retched and threw up a pinkish-amber liquid into the basin. The taste and smell of bile mixed with a kaleidoscope of flavors as his spirited indulgence at The Stray Cat lurched out of him.

"Good, good," the man behind him said. He turned the dial on the bathtub, and water poured from the spout. He pulled up the shower pin on the spout, and the water gurgled and stopped before spraying out from above. He pushed Nate's head under the stream. "Come to your senses. I need you to listen."

The cold water struck Nate's head. He lurched

backward, but the man pushed him back into the stream. Nate shook his head, spraying water around the bathroom like a wet mutt.

"No, wait, stop it! Fuck you!" He elbowed the man behind him and struggled to his feet, water dripping from his hair and down his face, soaking his gray T-shirt.

He looked over at the man. A shadow veiled half of the familiar lined face and thick gray hair. Recognition jolted Nate, boiling to a fresh fury. "*Dad?* What the hell are you…" He paused for a moment, the memories of the day rolling him over. He felt an icy drop in his stomach, his chest tightening. "Cheryl…" He gasped. "Dad, is she…" His throat constricted and he couldn't say more.

The older man shook his head, wincing. "No, no, she'll live." He stepped forward and put his hands on Nate's shoulders. "Listen to me. You can fix this."

Nate's eyes widened in shock under the harsh bathroom light. What he had taken as a shadow sharpened into puckered, pinkish-red scars that stretched along the left side of the man's face. "Oh my god, Dad… what happened to you?"

"I'm not *Dan*, goddammit." The man tightened his grip on Nate and shook him. "Can't you see? Peggy had it all figured out." He guided Nate out of the bathroom, let go, and stalked further into the main room. "Where's the journal? Still behind the books?" He looked at the bookshelf across the room, his eyes then dropping to the area near the front door.

Nate concentrated to steady himself. His head still swam but was clear enough to remember that the baseball bat was on the other side of the bed. He scanned the room for anything else he could use as a weapon. The man stood between him and the kitchen, his gaze focused on the shattered clock on the bloodied floor by the door while he frowned. As Nate contemplated rushing him, maybe pushing the older man aside so he could get to the kitchen for a knife, the man started shaking, almost vibrating, his form becoming less focused, blurring in and out.

"Ah, shit!" The man cried out and bent forward, shaking his head. "I've broken it. I gotta…" He looked at Nate and rushed toward him, grabbing Nate's shoulders. "You have to read the journal! Read everything Cheryl marked. It's all there. Everything you need to know! I'm the proof it works. *You're* the proof!"

Nate stared at him, his eyes wide, his mouth gaping as he shook his head.

"Dammit! Don't you see? I'm *you!* I'm you thirty years from now!" The man shook Nate by the shoulders. "Peggy had it all figured out! You can fix this! Make it so everything is…"

The man's features softened and diffused, his form losing detail until he became a gray shadow that collapsed in on itself, shrinking away to nothing. A cool breeze passed over Nate's wet hair and shirt as air rushed to fill the space where the man had stood. Nate shivered, the lingering ache from the man's grip the only evidence he had existed at all.

Nate didn't know how long he stood, his eyes fixed on the empty space where the man had been, before his knees buckled. The bed broke his fall, and he sat up on the sagging mattress, his eyes twitching, his mind a fog. Whatever thoughts came to him dissipated like the man had moments before, unable to grasp or comprehend what had just happened.

Out of habit, he glanced to where the bell jar clock had once stood, looking to see what time it was. The empty area by the door jolted his mind back. The memory of what happened earlier punched him in the gut, and he clutched to that memory, awful as it was, to pull him back to something he at least could grasp.

He stood up and stared at the wreckage on the floor. He felt his mouth stiffen to a frown, and he imagined he looked much like his visitor did moments before he seemed to dissemble and collapse to nothing. Nate's head throbbed.

A dream, Nate thought. *It had to be a dream. No, a hallucination.* He nodded to himself, convincing himself of its sense. *No more strange cocktails at The Stray Cat.*

Consoled, but not quite satisfied with his rationalization, he stepped over the mess, careful not to step his stockinged feet onto it or even look at it, and grabbed his cell phone off the desk. The time on the lock screen read 02:34. It was around ten thirty when he left the hospital. He had no idea when he left the bar, but it was now too late to go back for a couple of cold beers. His mouth felt dry at the thought, and he shook his head to clear it from his mind.

A chat balloon icon sat under the time display. Nate unlocked the screen and opened his messenger app to a message from his father, sent just after one in the morning. "Cheryl stable but unchanged. Visiting allowed in morning at ten, but she won't be awake. Room 401."

Nate put the phone back on his desk and took a deep breath. Hours to go before he could see his sister, and he was now too wide awake to try returning to sleep. Over the next hour, he kept himself busy, starting with cleaning the broken clock. He put on his shoes and tried to keep his mind blank, not thinking about what happened but focusing instead on the movements of the kitchen broom he used to sweep up the glass and brass pieces from the carpet before throwing them in a plastic trash bin. The end table the clock had sat upon had a broken leg, so it was trash as well. Nate took it and the bin of debris and placed them outside his front door. He would discard them in the complex dumpster when it was light outside.

By now his head throbbed with a queasiness in his stomach, what one of his AA cohorts referred to as "the whiskey flu." He put the broom back between the wall and refrigerator.

The stained carpet—*Don't think about why it is stained, bubba*—was not something he could clean. Instead, he grabbed a throw rug from the bathroom and placed it over the spot, the smell from the bathtub igniting his churning stomach. Satisfied the rug was enough for the spot, he returned to the bathroom and turned on the shower, rinsing out the basin before stripping and standing under the water. He turned the knob, first lukewarm, then cool, and then cold. Standing under the stream, he shivered, forgetting his headache and the night's ruin and fever dreams.

Nate dressed in a clean T-shirt and jeans and glanced at his phone's screen. It was just after three. Hours to go before he could get the car and visit Cheryl. He felt a buzzing of panic as he considered what to do to occupy himself. Glancing at his desk, he considered booting up his laptop and browsing the internet for mindless distractions. He sat in his desk chair, his eyes wandering to the bookshelf. The black binding of Aunt Peggy's journal peeked out from behind the row of books.

Peggy had it all figured out. You can fix this.

Nate felt a tug of curiosity coupled with a twinge of hope. What did he have to lose by burning through a few pages of the journal? At the very least, it was what Cheryl had wanted him to do. It was one of the last things she asked of him...

Nate grabbed the journal, careful not to disturb his neatly arranged books, and opened it to one of the pages Cheryl had marked. The pink sticky note she used as a bookmark had a pair of question marks scribbled on it. The page was a series of numerical triplets in parentheses, with what looked like time notations alongside them. A few pages later, his aunt had handwritten a series of letter-number variations, again with what looked like time stamps. He flipped further to another page Cheryl had marked.

Katherine wouldn't speak to me after Nate died.

"Ugh," Nate said to himself, looking up at the ceiling. "Peggy, what the hell is this?" He closed his eyes and sighed, remembering again what the man had said to him. "Oh, what the hell."

Nate looked back down at the journal and started reading the page from the beginning.

7

The Journal of Margaret Lynn Mayfield

To understand what has happened, I will write this down. I don't even know if I'll remember this over time, which is why I spent the past night writing my memorized specifications. But what if I forget what they are for? I have two wildly divergent memories, enough to drive anyone mad with the contradictions and inconsistencies. One set, I suspect, could fade. I now write the memories from that earlier reality as best I can, so I will have a record of what transpired in case the memory slips away.

Katherine wouldn't speak to me after Nate died. I fled the car as the fire approached, and it was unforgivable. To my shame, I didn't even think of the boy until she started crying out his name, after the young men, bystanders in the park, pushed past me and pulled her from the wreckage. Cut and mildly burned, her body would recover, but her son was dead.

Katherine ignored me during the funeral. I left after the service, not wanting to face her glare, not wanting to add to her grief. Over the next weeks, she wouldn't return my calls. I spoke to Dan, and he kept telling me she would come around eventually, that I just needed to be patient. But how could she forgive me? I left her child to burn alive in the car. It was unforgivable. I eventually stopped trying to reach out to them. I thought it best I fade from their lives.

I could not, however, escape what had happened. I berated myself constantly for my cowardice. What had that child felt as he struggled against the flames, crying for help while I stood dumbly outside. Did he see me standing there, unaware of him, knowing he had been forgotten? Knowing I had abandoned him?

The worst part was I had *forgotten* about him. In those moments after I escaped, I thought of only myself. It was as if my mind shut off, excluding everything but self-preservation from the moment of impact to that final conflagration consuming the car. I didn't think once of Nate in all that time. Not until Katherine started screaming his name into the roaring flames.

I returned to Chicago to bury myself in my research and teaching. Years passed as I focused on work my work and quest for tenure, which I proudly attained. To the *exclusion of all else, I continued to study, research, teach, and write papers. I let no one close. It was easier that way. I got more done. I refused to let myself reflect on my life before. I published research papers and books that received high acclaim. My existence was my vocation. I found great success in this strategy. Until I didn't. In a single moment, it all fell apart.*

Driving home from the university, a stack of papers to grade on the seat beside me fell over, and I cursed, reaching over to prevent the whole pile from scattering to the floor. As I slowed for a red light, I took my eyes off the road for just an instant, looking at the mess. I rear-ended the car that had already stopped in front of me. It was a minor fender-bender, nothing more than a firm tap from my almost-stopped car.

I couldn't breathe. It was as if I had returned to the morning of the terrible crash, the mild thump flashing to my mind how my body was thrown forward against the back of Katherine's seat, the smell of gasoline, the sight of smoke and then flames. It felt more than a memory but a return to that experience and all my failures.

The young woman in the car ahead of me got out, glanced at her fender and then walked over to my open window. I was shaking, my foot pressing on the brakes and my hands gripping the steering wheel. I was certain if I moved, I would die. She was kind, assuring me no damage done and then asking if I was okay. I only looked ahead, afraid to move. She reached in and touched my shoulder, and I shrieked. She called 911, and the paramedics arrived. After a bit, they determined I wasn't injured or having a stroke or other physical ailment. The woman stayed with me the whole time. Short dark hair and gold hoop earrings. I never got her name. After the panic subsided, I felt deep embarrassment. I drove myself home and thought nothing more would come of it.

I was wrong. My work suffered in the days following the incident. I couldn't let go of the memories, and I became distracted teaching my students, ending classes early as I lost my focus mid-lecture. My assistant, Kevin Whitaker, gently suggested I get help. He had experience with a therapist, Dr. Tina Kryzelnitski (she went by Dr. Tina), who successfully helped him with troubles related to his military experience. He gave me her information.

I won't go into much detail about my sessions with Dr. Tina, but her process was to start with talk therapy, cognitive-behavioral therapy, accompanied by a process of moving my eyes while describing my experience. The goal, she claimed, was to rewire my brain to accept the memory as in the past, not something to relive in the present. She used colored lights for my eyes to follow along a light bar she set up in front of me. She also played tones that sounded like Tibetan singing bowls, soft and oscillating in headphones from one ear to the other as my eyes followed the lights.

During one session, I recited my memories of the accident while Dr. Tina played the lights and tones, encouraging me to relive the experience with the belief I did the best I could in an impossible situation. As I focused on the lights and tones, envisioning the burning car as I stood outside, I experienced the most vivid recollection of the event since the minor fender-bender that reignited my guilt. I was standing by the car, feeling the heat, hearing the bystanders and approaching emergency vehicles. More surprising, I was standing behind my younger self, who stood there trembling and unmoving. I felt enormous contempt that she had a chance now, *before the flames got worse, to rescue her nephew. I yelled, "Do something!" and pushed her toward the car. I felt her weight against my hands, and she stumbled forward, reaching out for balance, and then shrieked as her hands reached the flames. She stumbled back, away from the flames, crying and holding her right hand. I cried out myself, remembering in that instant that someone* did *push me toward the burning car that morning, and the imagery vanished, replaced by Dr. Tina's light bar. I was safe in her office, feeling a swell of embarrassment for shouting. She quickly turned off the lights and tones and asked me what I was feeling.*

My shock over the vision fueled into anger. "Enormous frustration," I yelled at her, throwing off the headphones. "I let a child die, and nothing we do here can change that." My indulgence with therapy was doing nothing to erase the death for which I was responsible. I fled her office.

As my anger cooled, I reflected on the vividness of my vision. For those few seconds, I truly felt I was back there, next to the car. Something else occurred to me. I remembered paramedics treating my burned hand after someone pushed me toward the car. Yet I knew this had never happened! I stood on the sidelines as the car burned, too shocked and afraid to move, never getting too near. No one ever pushed me. I also remembered the jolt of a push toward the car, being burned and pulling back (I heard someone yelling, too, but with so much surrounding noise, I never heard actual words). I had a second-degree burn that gave me pain for weeks. But I also knew that never happened.

I looked at my hand. A shining pink scar covered the backside. Of course, I have always had this scar since the day of the accident. Yet, equally real to me, I knew I never received such a scar. I knew both things at once. The scar seemed to confirm I had been pushed, perhaps by a bystander trying to do what I could not, and I got in the way, but I was certain this was never the case before my session with Dr. Tina. How could this be possible? Perhaps the scar was a psychosomatic response from the therapy, but why did I remember getting the burn as if it had happened all those years ago?

I approached one of my closest university colleagues, Navenka Oyibo, who specialized in philosophy and metaphysics. I explained to her my experience and asked if it was possible I could have actually interacted for a few seconds in the past.

She looked at me quizzically. "You've always had the scar, Peggy."

She grabbed her cane and invited me to walk with her. Her thin form looked frail, but she walked at a brisk pace, using her cane only occasionally to correct her balance. She took me along the maze of campus pathways while we talked. I told her of my experience at the therapy session and my dual memories of that moment I reached out and received the burn, even as I also knew I did no such thing.

She walked silently beside me for a minute as we approached a fountain, slowly nodding, misted clouds overhead forming a halo-like rainbow. "Let me ask you something," she said. "What is this thing we call 'the past'?"

I felt a bit confounded at the question, for the answer was obvious, "Things that have happened."

"And how do you know these things have happened? Where are they?" She motioned with her cane at the large pool in front of the fountain and to the back end of sand-sculpted figures.

"Well, we see the effects, we grow older, we carry scars, we..." I paused, looking at a sculpted cloaked figure at the

front end of the fountain facing the procession of figures at the other end of the pool. "We remember what has happened."

"Ah," she said, "but those things are all observations now, in this present moment."

I looked at her and took a deep breath. "But they still happened."

"But," she said, "the past does not exist, does it, except as a memory in the present moment."

Glancing at the plaque at the foot of the cloaked figure, I understood why she had walked us here. We stood at The Fountain of Time. *"Okay."*

"My point is, the past does not exist at all. It is our own construct, something we use to explain our present memories, to explain the evidence of change we see in and around ourselves, from one present moment to the next." She stopped looking at the fountain and turned to me. "Now, I ask you, what is the future?"

I shrugged my shoulders. "What is to come?"

She nodded, and we began walking away from the fountain. "But it, too, does not exist. Does it? It is another human construct to predict what may come. It has no reality except as our thoughts in the present moment."

I laughed, not from humor but from exasperation. "Oh, Navenka, are you saying there is no past or future?"

"I am saying, Peggy, we can only live in the present moment, for past and future are memories and ideas,

imperfect constructions of what has been or will be. But now, I ask you, what do you think is this thing I call 'the present moment'?"

"You just told me. It is now. The point in which we live."

"Think carefully, now, Peggy." She stopped walking again and motioned to a bench. She sat down with a slight groan as I sat next to her. "What is the 'present moment'?" She leaned forward on her cane, looking out at the green lawns. "When does such a moment emerge from what we consider the future? In what instant does the present exist before it transforms into a part of the past?" She turned toward me. "How can we, mere humans, even measure such an instant?"

"Oh, Navenka," I said, "this all feels very existential. Are you saying that time, even the present moment in which we exist, is not real?"

"I am saying that we humans are trapped in this container we call 'time.' We are moving forward, our perception tells us, by the passage of one present moment to the next. Each of these successive moments are so infinitesimally small that they are beyond our ability to measure, if they even exist at all."

We sat silently for a few minutes. A flock of warblers soared overhead, passing over the lawns while calling out their own secret melody before they disappeared into the blue.

Finally, I gathered my courage to ask her, "Navenka, how does this relate to my experience?"

"Peggy," she said, "I've known you a long time. I know you have a troubling experience in your past that still haunts you, but I've never known you to engage in fantastical claims. So I don't believe you are now." She took my right hand and traced a finger over the edges of the scar. "Some theorize, or, more accurately, hypothesize, that the reason we cannot measure an instant of any present moment is because this illusion of time we are trapped in prevents it. In this train of thought, only one instance truly exists, a singularity of all existence, of all that was, all that is, and all that will ever be."

I looked at her, trying to grasp what she meant. "Are you saying everything that has or will happen is all occurring at the same moment?"

"I have always known you to have this scar," she said, still tracing around its edges. "Consider for a moment that you traveled back to your experience from years ago and did something different, and you carried that forward, changing what happened. In the hypothesis I explained, it could be possible to reach back within our own past, as it is still with you, happening through you, as part of this present instant within which we exist."

I felt a shiver through my spine, a warming vibration throughout my body as I considered the possibility. Did something happen to me through Dr. Tina's therapy techniques that allowed me to capture a moment of my history and make an actual, tangible change?

A carillon played from the tower of the university chapel, the sound echoing over the elms and oaks. I glanced at my watch: six o'clock in the evening. Navenka stood up and stretched her back. I stood, and we began walking back to the hall of the Department of Philosophy. I talked little on the way back, my mind absorbing what she had told me. We reached the steps to her hall's ivy-framed wooden doors.

"Navenka," I said. "If this really happened, if I somehow traveled back to that morning, I want to figure out how it worked. Help me..."

She cut me off with a wave of her cane. "No, Peggy! Abandon this idea! You risk meddling with the machines of the cosmos, those mechanisms beyond our human understanding that shape all existence. We must bear the burdens of the trauma machine that guides our lives. It gifts us our sufferings so they may produce perseverance, and through perseverance the character we need to fulfill our role in the universal fabric. Meddling in that could create unintended sufferings beyond the sphere of your small life, clipping a thread that unravels a whole design. Consider yourself lucky if your brief sojourn resulted only in a change to yourself!"

Her tone took me aback. I stood with my mouth open, and her face told me this conversation was over. We bid *our farewells, but just before she ascended the stone steps, she grasped my hand and said, "Peggy, my harshness is only partly from the danger a pursuit of this nature poses, both its formidable potential and what the mere exploration itself might do to you and to your career. But also..." She paused, leaning on her cane. "I've studied these concepts for most of my life, and if what you believe happened actually did, I truly envy you."*

* * *

I slept little that night, nor during the months that followed. I could see no purpose in the death of a child, nor accept my role in it. If there was even a chance I could set this right, I had to try. I was allowed a peek into the potential for doing this. Wouldn't that make this quest part of the "cosmic design" Navenka spoke about?

I couldn't convince Navenka to help me, so I tried to engage Dr. Tina in the possibility, begging her to try the process on me again to see if I could repeat my experience. She refused, explaining as a psychotherapist she believed my interpretation of the experience proved I was not a suitable subject for her technique. She referred me to a colleague, instead, and I felt rejected and desperate. I approached her another time soon after, but I was not kind to her when she again refused. She responded to my angry words that I was not to consult her again.

So began my quest to repeat the experience on my own. I purchased my own light bar and downloaded music files of Tibetan singing bowls. I spent weeks running the lights and sounds, meeting with abject failure for my efforts. The more I failed, the more desperate but determined I became. I could save the boy I let die if I just could get back there again.

I believed Navenka's ideas about time, for they were my only hope to make what I destroyed whole again. It had to be possible, for I knew in the deepest recesses of my soul that I created the scar on my hand years after the event. It was a genuine experience. I had changed the past. I needed to do so again. I needed to save Nate from the unthinkable death my negligence brought to him.

I spent the entire summer on my obsession, to no avail. A new semester would start in a few weeks, and I had done no planning or preparation for my responsibilities. I began spending most nights in my office at the university, trying to scramble building my course work while also continuing my work with lights and sonics.

Kevin found me in my office asleep at my desk while the light bar throbbed and bell tones played from speakers attached to an MP3 player. He had been taking photographs of a new collection of artifacts for the religion department with his Polaroid camera, and he set his satchel containing it on my file cabinet and woke me up. He insisted on taking me to my apartment, and after a brief argument, I acquiesced. I turned off my light bar and music and he, to his credit, didn't ask me about it.

The next morning I returned to my office determined to get rid of the light bar and forget about my attempts to do the impossible. I had a onetime experience and, whether it was real or not, I had to accept I would never experience it again. It was time to focus again on my work and let the past remain distant memories. I couldn't help but feel I had failed Nate again.

When I entered my office, I found a stack of photographs on my desk next to Kevin's camera. Each photograph was of a page of a stenographer's spiral tablet, like I used to make notes. In fact, the writing looked like my own, but I had no recollection of writing any of these figures of parenthetical numeric triplets. They looked like formulas, about thirty pages of them, and as I shuffled through each photo, I came across one that made me dizzy with shock.

I sat in my chair and stared at it, barely able to comprehend what I was seeing. The photograph was of me, the stack of cards fanned out in my grip like a hand of playing cards. I stood off-center, cutting off half my face, as if I had taken the photograph myself using my other hand. Behind my image, the wall calendar was still marked for the day before, and the clock next to it revealed the photo was taken after two in the morning.

I turned this Polaroid photograph over and, scribbled in black ink, was a note in my handwriting: "Kevin will build it. This will work!" Then some instructions on what the numbers on each photographed page meant.

After getting over my shock, I considered what could explain the photographs. The most reasonable explanation I could devise was that, in my obsessive fever, I sleepwalked to my office and took the photographs. If that were the case, however, where were the pages of formulas the photographs contained? I found no such writing in any of my notebooks. Even if my sleepwalking self had discarded them, surely I would remember writing them down. Or did I write them in my sleep as well? Then why were there only photographs of these notes? Why didn't I just leave myself the actual notes?

A fantastical alternative was that a future version of myself had somehow come upon the proper formulations of light and sound to successfully travel to the past, and she did exactly that in order to give me the specifications. Perhaps she brought the notes with her, and perhaps she couldn't just leave them as they would return to her own time with her. I also wondered why she didn't just meet me, granting me incontrovertible proof that time travel was possible?

I could only speculate. But what I had were specifications and instructions to give Kevin to build a device of some sort. That was enough to get me working.

The text in the photographs was legible, if a bit small, so I transcribed the specifications so Kevin could read *them more easily. This took me several hours, and with my hand aching and my eyes tired, I pressed too hard on the paper and broke off the tip of my pen, leaving behind a blotch of black ink. To my surprise, the mark matched exactly an ink spot on the page in the photograph. This proved to me that, indeed, the pages I wrote I would one day deliver to myself in the past.*

Of course, this begged an enigma I could not ignore nor ever solve. If I gave myself the specifications I would later travel back to give myself, where did these specifications actually originate?

8

Nate snapped the journal shut and leaned back in his chair, staring at the dust motes on the popcorn-textured ceiling. *This is the weirdest shit I ever read,* he thought. But so was his vivid encounter just an hour before. He stood up and stretched, glancing at his phone's screen. Just after three thirty. Too much time ahead to just sit around his apartment doing nothing.

She mentioned specifications. For what? She mentioned a device. What sort of device? He sat back down and flipped through the journal to the pages with the parenthetical formulas. Numerical triplets separated by commas. They had to be color codes in RGB format. The time codes in front of them might indicate the length, perhaps in seconds and milliseconds. Each line had a set of paired numbers. They looked like positioning ratios. Then a number followed, in some cases, by a triplet or quartet of numbers. Finally, some lines had another triplet of positive and negative numbers. But the RGB had to represent the colored lights of a light bar she had written about. Like these numbers were specifications to recreate the experience she had with her shrink.

What if he could write up a quick programming code to display the colors on his laptop's screen? He used to be a whiz at coding, building and supporting applications for McVey Land and Living before too many missed and tardy days got him fired and he had to refurbish laptops to sell to make some cash.

This wouldn't be a complicated programming job. Each row of numbers was consistent in format. He could build a table, maybe use an OCR app on his cell phone to convert Peggy's handwriting into text, so he didn't have to type it all out.

Nate photographed the pages with the specifications on his cell phone and then imported them to his laptop, making corrections where the OCR didn't translate correctly. He coded a simple looping routine to read the columns of the table he made for time, color, and position on the laptop screen. How did she have Kevin build this for her? Was this what he did?

Nate sat back and sighed. She never had Kevin, whoever he was, build her anything. A teacher's assistant? She hadn't worked at the university in almost twenty years.

Yet someone who looked a lot like him had dragged him out of bed just a couple of hours earlier and vanished into thin air. Could it be true? More likely, he was losing his mind, just like his aunt did. Maybe something contagious was in the journal. Maybe Cheryl caught it, too...

Nate rocked his head. *Cheryl.* His heart sank as he thought of her lying in the hospital, hooked up to god knows what. *You can fix this*, the man had told him. If there was even a slight chance of it being true...

"Awe, what the hell," Nate said, and he clicked the program to run.

It worked. Lights flashed in a colorful display at various points on his laptop's screen. He stared into the lights, concentrating. Maybe he could have an experience like Aunt Peggy claimed in her therapy session. Maybe he could find himself back at the night before and pull Rico away from Cheryl when it mattered most.

After twenty minutes, Nate turned the program off. Nothing. Nada. Zip. What a waste of time.

Nate put on his sneakers and grabbed a jacket

and his keys. A few beers would help him get back to sleep or at least numb him from all that had happened, and he still had a half hour to purchase alcohol at the market before the 4 a.m. cutoff. TJ's Minute Mart was just a ten-minute walk.

The night air felt good against his face, and he felt peaceful under the familiar trees and clear sky shimmering with stars above.

Moments later, he approached the market's glass doors, passing a graffiti-scarred phone booth that reeked of stale urine, the receiver dangling limply over the sidewalk. A harsh buzz greeted him as the market doors slid open. Nate nodded at the cashier, a bored-looking middle-aged man with greasy salt-and-pepper hair. He glanced at Nate and then returned to flipping through pages of a travel magazine.

Nate approached the refrigerated beer cabinet and looked through the glass at his options. His eyes glazed past the Samuel Adams selection, moving past Sierra Nevada, Michelob, Budweiser, Miller Light, and finally settling on a twelve-pack of Coors Light. He opened the glass door and put his hand on the package, hesitating just a moment as he considered how hard he had fallen off the wagon. Hell, even the crowd at AA would give him a break under the circumstances, although he had to brush over the fact he started drinking before Cheryl's injury. Red coin be damned, he could start again some other night. Right now, he needed the escape it promised, if nothing else. He pulled the case off the shelf.

As he approached the checkout, his right-hand fingers gripping the twelve-pack handle, he passed a wire rack of travel games. *Travel Bingo, Hangman, Magnetic Chess and Checkers,* various crosswords, and other game books. One caught his eye, *Advanced Musical Game Book.* The colorful cover showed music-themed crosswords, word search, and connect-the-dots. Nate chuckled to himself. *What kind of nerd would play* this *on a road trip?*

Then he remembered Cheryl making fun of him for bringing a book on computer programming for beginners when he was twelve (Aunt Peggy insisted they leave electronic devices at home, so he picked the book as a protest but found it more interesting than he expected), so maybe some kid would discover his music genius by picking this up. He started to turn from the rack when he glanced back at the musical game book. It had the declaration of "Over 150 Puzzles!" surrounded by colorful musical notes, and eye-rolling banners that proclaimed "Adventures with Ambrose Piano Tabs" and "Knockabout with Klavar Notation" and "Meander through MIDI," the last of which had a colorful series of numeric formulas that caught Nate's eye.

They looked familiar. He took the book in his free hand as it dawned on him. These were like the odd number combinations in Aunt Peggy's journal! She mentioned tones along with the lights. Could those numbers she wrote be MIDI musical notations, which Nate recalled from his school days stood for Musical Instrument Digital Interface? When did she learn something like that? Well, why not? Stranger things had happened, like being pulled from bed by an older man claiming to be him in thirty years.

Nate stared at the cover for another moment and then returned to the refrigerated shelf and put back the beer. If her crazy story was real, he had to do what he could to find out. Better than drinking himself into another stupor to kill the long hours before he could visit Cheryl at the hospital.

He pulled a Red Bull variety pack from a shelf. He had a few hours to kill, and a caffeine buzz would get him through the rest of the night and help him concentrate. *You can fix this,* the man told him. Maybe this was the ticket. Worth a shot. Even if it came to naught, he'd be no worse off for the effort.

The cashier grunted as he looked at the game book, scanning its barcode into the register.

"Plannin' a wild night?" He chuckled, putting the game book in a thin plastic bag. Nate felt his face redden and shrugged his shoulder as the man scanned the Red Bull. He threw down two twenties and grabbed his change in silence, gripping the bag and case of Red Bull has he resisted the brief impulse to flip the man off. It didn't matter. As he hurried to his apartment, he felt something he hadn't in a long time—eager anticipation.

When he got back to his complex a few minutes later, he passed twinkling Christmas lights bordering his neighbor's window. *Tarsha is working tonight.* His neighbor made her living hooking up with men online, the lights a signal to find her apartment. As he passed, he could hear the rustling of sheets through the screen of the slightly parted window, the grunts of a customer inside the dark room. Nate scoffed, hoping her night job didn't attract the cops again.

Inside his apartment, he ripped open the puzzle book and examined the section on MIDI musical notes, disappointed it was just a few games with only a basic game to link each number (out of 128) to a specific note. The answer key, however, showed

Nate how the numbers worked, each one representing a note, but the triplets and quartets of number were chords. If nothing else, the puzzle book confirmed to him that these were what Aunt Peggy's code specified for the tonal elements of the device.

Nate downed a can of Red Bull and examined his laptop. He had coding software installed from ages ago that he would use for the basic program. To his relief, he also had a MIDI controller software he could tap into for the sounds. He chose a sound file called "meditation drone" that he imagined was close enough to a Tibetan singing bowl. A rush of energy from the drink made him lightheaded but hyperalert. Over the next hour, he downed two more of the drinks as he coded, his mind sharper than he'd felt in months. His heart beat fast, and his mind felt on fire as his fingers flicked along the keyboard with a sense of joy he hadn't felt from a coding project in years. It beat drowning himself in a case of beer.

After ninety minutes, he had the program finished. So simple, really. Nothing too complicated. He compiled the code as an app, naming it "PeiPei.exe."

He glanced at his cell phone clock. Just after six o'clock. The past two hours had flown by in what felt like less than half an hour. Doubt crested over him as his finger trembled on the mouse clicker to set the program to run. "Here goes nothing," he breathed and clicked.

The laptop's screen turned to black, and then the notes started playing as points of colored lights flickered across the screen. He stared into it, thinking of Aunt Peggy following the light bar and focusing on a time and place. He thought of Cheryl, concentrating on her arrival at his apartment the evening before. The chiming sounds continued and, to Nate's surprise, when they hit a specific set of chords, he felt a warm vibration flow down his spine. Something seemed to illuminate in his brain. He felt his eyes grow heavy, the lights dancing before him. He felt at peace.

A half hour later, he turned it off. The program did nothing but play random tones and flash colored lights, leaving him relaxed but exhausted. The program was just a meditation lamp, or the Red Bull was wearing off.

He slammed the laptop lid down and sat back in his chair. He stood up and stretched, his foot kicking four cans of Red Bull. He didn't remember drinking that many, but what else was new? His stomach growled, and he ate some cereal in the kitchen with another can of the energy drink.

He felt revitalized and wondered if he had missed something. The specs still had numbers he didn't understand. What if they were important? Did Aunt Peggy describe the device? Maybe that would reveal something. Nate sat back down at his desk and picked up the journal. Flipping a few pages ahead from where he had last read, his eyes fell upon a passage.

Kevin finished constructing the device in early October. About the size of a breadbox, he built it out of wood and painted it a glossy back, with an interior of circuits, wires to the lights, and a small synth card for the tones and a space for batteries. I understood none of the interior, but when he closed the lid, it looked quite elegant. A red switch on the right side turned it on or off, and each side had a speaker to play the tones. He also included a headphone jack, if I preferred that. He placed the lights positioned on its face as I had instructed, along with the spindles that jutted out from each side like the whiskers of a cat or the spindly legs of an arachnid that lay on its back. He referred to it as a "twonky," which I didn't understand. He said it was from an old science-fiction story he once read about a device of unusual origin. It seemed appropriate, but given the cat-like whiskers and elegant whimsy of the device's look, I told him I would call it my jabberwock. He tilted his head. "Juggernaut?" I laughed and corrected him, unaware of the prescience of his mistake.

Nate flipped back a few pages. *Cat whiskers?* This gave him an idea, and he looked at the pages with all the numbers. The triplet and quartets combinations he couldn't figure out suddenly made sense. The multiple numbers could be three-dimensional axis points. The device needed lights on the sides as well as the front.

The thought triggered a recent memory of when he visited Aunt Peggy after she started acting strange. She wept at the sight of him, embracing him in a desperate hug. Behind her, a web of multicolored lights twinkled, surrounding her desk chair.

Was that why she had hung the lights? A glow of renewed excitement jolted through him. He would need LED lights. He scrambled to his closet and pulled out his electronics box, where he kept anything he thought might be of use for his computer refurbishing projects. He came across no lights, but found some microcontrollers and USB plugs he could manipulate to connect to the laptop and control the lights, if he could find any.

An idea occurred to him. He took the materials to his desk and then looked out his front window. His neighbor's Christmas lights twinkled through colorful soft fades. Perfect. Maybe Tarsha would give them to him for cash. He grabbed a twenty out of his wallet and then walked along the breezeway to her door. Her window was slightly parted, and he heard a dual snoring, she and her trick down for the night.

He considered knocking on her door, but he knew from prior experience that waking her would put him on her shit list. He listened to the snoring through the gap in the window and then got another idea. Looking around to ensure no one was near, he reached in the open gap of the window and wrapped his index finger and thumb around the cord. Slowly, he pulled on it, the adhesive tape attaching the cord to the window giving way, section by section, as he pulled it out. He heard movement on the bedsprings inside and stopped, holding his breath.

He was twenty feet from his front door and prepared to dash inside if anyone spoke, but the movements inside calmed down, and he heard the snoring duet begin again. Nate took a deep, slow breath and finished detaching the lights from the inside of the window. One good tug and he might get it unplugged. He counted to himself, one... two... three... then pulled. The cord came loose with a snap as the prongs hit the glass and then the window frame, and something inside crashed to the floor with a shatter.

Nate ran to his apartment and, gripping the stolen string of LEDs, shut the door as quickly and quietly as possible before dousing his apartment lights. He peeked out his front window, hearing Tarsha exclaiming, "Mother fucker...shit!" Then her door opened.

Nate ducked out of view, his heart racing. An uncontrollable giggling struck him, and he bit his finger to shut it down. He heard Tarsha swear again and then her door slam followed a moment later by the sharp sound of her window sliding shut.

After a minute, he turned the lights back on and, gripping his stolen LEDs, went to his kitchen and grabbed a pair of scissors. Time to get to work.

Having worked with the guts of dozens of laptops, the task took him just over an hour. He clipped the cord of LEDs into sections and then attached them to the stiff thin metal of a few wire hangers he cut up as a sacrifice for his project. He used a soldering iron to connect the wires to the microcontrollers and cannibalized a couple of old flash drives to create USB connectors to attach to the microcontrollers so they could plug into the laptop. Once finished, it looked like something out of a science-fiction horror film.

As Nate recoded the program to account for the new sets of lights, the closed curtains over his windows became haloed by growing light. It was just past eight thirty in the morning when he finished.

Nate patted the leather binding of Aunt Peggy's journal. "Well, Pei-Pei, here it goes." He clicked the app into action.

As before, the lights flashed on the screen in colorful twinkling. To his relief, the peripheral lights also illuminated, and he leaned forward in his chair, his hands on his elbows, staring at the lights as the tones played. As before, after a minute, the chords started sending a warm tremor down his spine. He leaned forward, the lights twinkling with the chiming resonances seeming to draw him closer in.

He thought of lunch with Cheryl, coming home. If he went back to that moment, he could take his lunch, and she'd never come back for him later. None of the awful events that night would ever have happened. The timbre of the music pulsed through him, and Nate felt a sensation flowing under his skin. A shimmering, like a silvery warmth that trembled and then throbbed throughout his body. His eyes stared ahead, the lights seeming to disassociate from the laptop, floating in front and around him all on their own.

Wow. He wasn't sure if he spoke or thought the

word, but he felt weightless, his chair and desk gone. He floated.

He opens his eyes. A dust web drifts in the popcorn ceiling over his bookshelf. He feels enormously calm. Leaning forward, he squints his eyes against the sunlight glinting between the curtain panels over his desk. Nate blinks. "What the…"

He jumps up, but a fierce dizziness from the blood rushing to his legs forces him to sit back down.

He knocks the sides of his head with his fists. He is late for getting to the hospital, for seeing Cheryl. "Stupid, Nate, stupid, stupid."

He spent the entire night working on the idiot project, exhausting himself to sleep through the whole day. And nothing to show for it. He is still here, in his apartment, like nothing has happened. Maybe he missed something else in the specifications.

He reaches for Aunt Peggy's journal, but his hand meets with air. It isn't on his desk. Nate swivels in the chair, looking at the stained carpet to see if it had fallen. Maybe he put it back behind the books? He can't remember. Indeed, his memory of the night is now mostly a muddle. He reaches to the bookshelf, lifting himself out of the chair, but wooziness overcomes him and he falls forward, grabbing at the shelves to break his fall. His hands grasp some books, and they tumble to the floor with him, his head knocking against the wood and shaking the shelves as he feels a sharp pain to his head when something flat and stiff hits him. The framed photograph of him, Cheryl, and Peggy.

Nate shakes his head. "Goddammit, get your head together," he hisses to himself, rubbing his head and examining a small amount of blood on his fingers. He shakes his head to clear his mind and then kicks the books away. Rubbing his head with one hand, he picks up the photograph with the other. On the back is a note, a tag from a Christmas gift three years ago. In Peggy's handwriting, he reads, "To my favorite nephew. Love, Pei-Pei." It's a family joke, as he is her *only* nephew, and he kept the note as a keepsake attached to the back of the frame.

Nate slowly picks himself up off the floor, the picture in his hands, and sits down on the bed. *What happened, Pei-Pei,* he thinks. *What really happened to you?* He closes his eyes, the soft ticking by the front door calming. *If only...*

Ticking? Nate's eyes flash open. Across from him,

standing on a small table by the front door, is the bell jar clock.

Nate stands up and walks to the clock. He sees his warped reflection on the curved glass. He sets the note from Peggy down on the small table and touches the glass, running his fingers over its cool, smooth surface as if nothing had happened to it. The carpet is in its usual ratty condition at his feet with no evidence of the awful thing that happened on this spot.

Or happened *yet*? Nate feels a chill run down his back. Did the program work? Actually *work*? Nate looks over at his desk. His laptop sits in its place, the lid closed, no microcontrollers or wired LED lights flaring out from its sides. Because he hasn't coded it yet. He hasn't yet built his own... what did his aunt call it? His own jabberwock.

His eyes scan across his apartment. He senses it in a detailed, hyperawareness. His bed is neatly made but slightly wrinkled from where he sat and placed the framed photograph, the kitchen's scuffed and burned countertops, the floor swept and mopped, as clean as any twenty-year-old linoleum can be. The beige carpet is the same, stained and flattened with paths to the kitchen and bathroom from occupants over the decades, but as clean as he has ever made it with a stiff kitchen broom.

"Aunt Peggy, you clever gal, it actually works!" He smiles and feels present, truly *here*, his thoughts focus on the air around his skin, the stillness of the room, the cushion of the carpet against his stockinged feet...

Nate looks down. No shoes. He isn't wearing his sneakers, only his thin athletic socks. He glances toward his desk chair. He was wearing the shoes, he is certain of it, when he started the program.

As he ponders this, a car rumbles outside his front window. He looks out the part in the curtains. Cheryl's car is stopping in front of his unit. The passenger-side door opens and someone gets out.

Nate gasps. It is *him* getting out of the car. Behind him, his sister sits behind the wheel. Nate touches the table to steady himself as his other self closes the car door, harsh and loud, and then approaches the front door. His other self pauses at the door, turns around, and then faces the door again and kicks it.

A cold thunderbolt ignites in Nate's chest. What would he say? What would his *other self* say if he opens the door to find himself standing there? Keys jangle as the locks on the door turn and click. Nate, panicked, turns and runs, dashing to the bathroom and shutting the door.

He listens. He hears the door opening, the hum of traffic from the street. Shaking and trying to steady his breath, he feels lightheaded and reaches for the wall to steady himself, grabbing a towel instead that, when he tries grabbing it for balance, falls to the floor and knocks over a small white trash can. He falls against the wall to stop himself from tumbling to the floor.

"I've got a gun!"

He hears his own voice shouting from the other room. Nate jumps, now knowing what is happening on the other side. He scrambles to the bathtub and slides open the narrow window above it, his only chance for escape. He hoists himself up, cursing himself for not thinking of locking the bathroom door. He pushes on the black security bars outside the window. To his relief, they fall away easily with a metallic thud to the dirt below. He pulls himself through the narrow opening, grateful he is small and thin enough to fit, and wrestles himself over the edge. As gravity takes over, he feels a hand grabbing at his foot, but he tumbles through.

He breaks the fall with his hands, his legs and feet thumping against the outside wall, the brackets of the iron security bars inches from his face. Hearing his earlier self on the other side of the wall, Nate scrambles back up, kicking the bars out of his way, and runs, rocks stinging through his thin socks. He looks down to avoid stepping on any of the various shards of amber, green, and clear glass that stud the ground in the back of his building. He rounds the corner and continues running toward the sidewalk. He absorbs what has just happened. He saw Cheryl... and his own self from the day before... and as the incredibleness of it sinks in, a pulling sensation emerges deep inside, expanding outward, and the world around him unravels...

Nate moved forward, the chair slipping out from under him as his legs continued in their desperate run. His balance lost, he grabbed at his desk as he fell forward, crying out as he knocked his head against the edge and then stumbled to the floor, his chair clattering behind him.

He rubbed his forehead and sat on the floor. His feet ached, and he pulled off his sneakers and socks. He rubbed his feet, his fingers running over indentations and light cuts. He then felt through his hair along his scalp until he came to an area of dried blood.

Maybe he hurt his head and feet during his frantic, almost fugue state as he assembled the computer program and peripherals. He could have knocked against a closet shelf getting his electronics box. He might have stepped his sock-clad feet into the broken glass and metal of the clock before he cleaned up the floor by the front door.

He put his socks and shoes back on and then stood up to pull the framed photograph off the bookshelf. The note he had on the back was not there. Yet he knew it had been on the day before, after his experience with the burglar, he was certain of it. During his experience, however, he left it on the table next to the clock.

Nate rushed out his front door and, squinting in the bright morning light, and looked into the plastic trash bin he placed there the previous night. He rummaged through it, careful not to cut himself on the broken glass, looking for the note. If he had left it on the table during his experience, it must be in this debris somewhere. After a moment, he pulled out the thick piece of paper with a snowman on it. The tag from Aunt Peggy. *To my favorite nephew...*

"Yes!" Nate jumped up, gripping the note in his hand. "It worked! It fucking worked!" He knew with certainty that not only had he traveled back in time, but he had effected changes that hadn't happened before.

He put the trash bin back outside and placed the tag near the photo on his shelf. Then he sat back at the computer. He would run the program again and return to a moment when he could prevent Rico from hurting Cheryl.

The screen remained blank as he ran his fingers along the touch mouse panel. He poked some keys, but the screen didn't change. Then a brief display of a battery icon appeared with a red line and stating zero percent.

Damn. Nate picked up the cord to the A/C charger. He had unplugged it when he needed to attach the microcontrollers because their large size covered the power connector jack. Now, he would need to charge the laptop before he could run the program again. He disconnected the microcontroller from the left side and then plugged in the power. The laptop screen flashed a battery icon with the word "Charging."

Nate looked at the clock on his phone's lock screen, surprised to see it was only nine o'clock. From the time he ran the program, experienced hiding from himself in the past, and rummaged through the box, he felt at least an hour had passed, but it had only been thirty minutes. Perhaps the journey back was instantaneous, regardless of how much time he spent in the prior time.

The laptop would take a while to charge, and he still needed to walk to The Stray Cat to get the car and visit Cheryl at ten. He could run the program again when he got back.

Nate quickly combed his hair, noting he was pale with dark rings under his eyes. He was hungry but could find something to eat at the hospital. He grabbed his wallet, locked his front door, and then began his walk to get the car.

As he walked in the golden light, the overnight chill still in the air, he felt a deep hope growing inside. Even if she wouldn't hear him, he looked forward to telling Cheryl that Aunt Peggy wasn't crazy; she was *right*. And Nate would do just as his older self asked him. He would make things right again.

9

The walk to The Stray Cat took Nate forty-five minutes, his feet stinging from the minor cuts he got running through rough terrain in his socks during his... how could he refer to it? He pondered this as he walked, settling on *time slip*. He slipped back in time, sans sneakers, which he would ask his future self about if he should ever encounter him again. He hoped that would not be necessary, especially considering the older man's scarred face. He didn't want to know how that happened, and he hoped what he did to save Cheryl would be enough to prevent further calamity.

This brought other questions to Nate's mind. If he went to the trouble to goad Nate into fixing things, why couldn't he have helped Cheryl himself? Were there limits to time travel? Could Nate's brief adventure preclude him from another attempt to return to that point in time? Too soon or too late, he might not be able to help Cheryl at all.

He was right there, at the right time and place, to do something, and he ran away to remain unseen. A heavy pall fell over him as he realized he could have dashed out the door, waving his arms before his other self got out of the car, reminding him to *get your fucking lunch.* Sure, it would have been awkward, but Cheryl wouldn't have returned later and everything would have been fine.

Yeah, Nate thought, *or Cheryl would have crashed the car into his building out of shock and god knows what would have come of that.*

It didn't matter. He had to go back and fix things, and he would figure out the way to do it. First, he had to see his sister.

He approached Cheryl's car in the potholed and gravelly parking lot of the bar, the champagne paint faded and scuffed. The windows were spotted from a brief overnight rain, but looked undisturbed after its overnight stay. Nate, relieved, half expected it to be propped up on cement bricks. He unlocked the door and got inside, struck by the warm interior and musty echo of his forgotten and discarded pasta lunch, the odor still a lingering ghost. He started the engine.

The drive to Saint Teresa's took another forty-five minutes, unusually long for the distance, but traffic remained heavy with work day commuters and one fender-bender being moved out of the traffic lanes. Parking at the hospital also took longer than the night before with Nate circling the parking lot twice before finding a spot to pull into.

He walked at a brisk pace, despite a mild limp from the stinging in his feet, double-checking his father's message from the night before for the room number. He didn't look forward to seeing his father again, but felt buoyed by his earlier experience. It didn't matter what Dad did, said, or thought. Nate could change things, so none of this happened. Aunt Peggy somehow saved his life, and later he would restore Cheryl's.

He rode the elevator up with an elderly pair of men, one in a wheelchair, who got off on floor three. Nate sighed with impatience, hitting the button to close while the doors paused open, and then shuddered with slow deliberation as they closed. The cab moved up another floor and the doors parted.

Nate glanced at a sign posted on the wall indicating the direction of rooms 400–420, his chest lurching at the tag in red text declaring "Neurological Intensive Care Unit (Neuro ICU)."

He followed the descending room numbers, glancing through glass and propped doors where bedridden patients lay attached to various machines with their forlorn loved ones around them. Nate slowed down as he approached his sister's room, not sure how he would feel seeing Cheryl in such a condition. Just then, his father entered the corridor, and Nate ran around the corner of an empty lobby station so he wouldn't see him. His father passed through some large metal doors leading to the south lobby. Nate hoped he was heading to the cafeteria downstairs. That would give him some time alone with his sister.

Once his father was out of sight, Nate continued down the corridor to room 401 and walked inside.

He seemed to have entered the wrong room. The face of the woman in the bed was puffy with dark rings around her eyes. A translucent tube was attached to her face, her chest rising in slow movements to the hiss and yawn of nearby machines. IVs snaked to her arms, attached to various mechanical boxes with blinking lights and beeping sounds. For an instant, Nate thought of his jabberwock and then shivered. The recognition of his sister dawned slowly, but it was her, now frail and still.

A wretched lump formed in Nate's throat as his

eyes stung. He crossed his arms, his hands gripping into fists. Anything he intended to say vanished from his mind. He stood, mute, before his supine and helpless little sister.

"She doesn't know we're here."

Nate whirled around toward the voice. Rico sat in a plastic chair in a shadowed corner near the door, leaning forward, his face pale in his cell phone's glow.

"What..." Nate's voice failed him and he tried again. "What are you doing here?"

"I don't want her to be alone." Rico checked his watch. "Been here a couple of hours. Well, an hour in the lobby before they'd let us up, but been here since ten." He looked at Nate, his bruised eye almost swollen shut. "You just missed your dad."

Nate felt a hot bolt of anger electrify his body. "Fuck you, Rico!" Nate's mouth twisted as he pushed away tears by raising his voice. "She wouldn't be here if it wasn't for you!"

Rico stood up. "Shut up, man." He took a step toward Nate and looked down at him. "I think you're confused. She tried to keep you from falling onto your drunk ass, and you pulled away and threw her off balance."

"What?" Nate looked up at Rico's face. "You *pushed her.*"

Rico stepped back, raising his scarred left hand to his forehead. "Oh, bro, no... no. How can you say that?" He put his hand down and slouched against the wall. "I covered for you with your dad, and you..."

Nate cut him off. "You pushed her and ran off instead of calling an ambulance!"

"I called the ambulance, dude! I couldn't call on my own phone. I wasn't even supposed to be there. I rushed to T.J.'s and used that rank pay phone..." He paused, shaking his head. "And what were *you* doing while she bled out? You crawled along the floor like a drunk dog, bawling and hiding under your desk!"

Nate clutched his hands into fists, his eyes burning as the muscles in his legs cracked like whips, propelling him toward Rico with his arms raised and ready to smash into the young man's face.

As he lunged forward, muscular arms wrapped around Nate's waist, pulling him back. He stumbled, nearly losing his balance as another man pulled him in a tight grip.

"Whoa, whoa, young man," a gravelly voice said in Nate's ear. "You come with me."

The man wore a blue face mask over his nose and mouth. Dressed in black jeans and a leather jacket, the man looked like security, sporting a bronze badge on his jacket front.

Rico looked relieved as the man pulled Nate from the room, holding Nate in front of him while gripping his arms as he walked him down the corridor. Nate turned his head, glimpsing the purple-pink scars that spread up from the mask's upper edge.

"What the fuck," Nate said, pushing against the man's strength and struggling to keep his balance. People looked out from the rooms they passed until the man pushed Nate into a custodian's closet and shut the door.

"Shut up, Nate," the older man said. "I just spared you five thousand bucks and three months in the big house."

Nate fell against the back wall, knocking over a mop that clattered to the floor.

The other man flipped on a light switch and removed the face mask. "That's better," he said, closing his eyes and breathing in deeply. Dark lines under his eyes faded, the deep age lines on his face growing more shallow. He opened his eyes and smiled. "You see, I had it easier now. *You'll* have it easier."

"Who are you?" Nate's voice emerged as a whisper.

"I told you, I'm *you*, thirty years from now. God,

wasn't it only last night for you? For me, it's been months since we met."

Nate shook his head, still unwilling to comprehend.

"You know the McVeys don't let things go. I... you, once upon a time... socked Rico a good one back there. Broke the asshole's jaw. He and his daddy prosecuted. Blamed me for the black eye, too. I got off easy, just three months at the Heights. Could have been *years*, considering McVey's lawyers, but the judge gave it to me easy. Still, try finding a decent job with a record. I just spared you that. And me."

Nate swallowed. "I don't have a fucking idea what you're talking about."

The older man let out an exasperated sigh. "Yeah, you've only had a taste of what is possible with the jabberwock. I don't have time to explain here." He reached out a hand and grasped Nate's arm. "Come on, I'll fill you in on the way. We have things to do."

10

The man pulled out a face mask like he was wearing from his jacket pocket. He took off his leather jacket as well and handed both to Nate. "Here, put these on."

Nate took the items. "Why?"

The older man put his mask back on. "So we aren't spotted. Dan is around somewhere. Do you really want him recognizing you and starting a conversation? I mean, sometimes I miss the man, but that could get more than a bit awkward."

Nate wondered why he would miss his father but then thought better of asking. Instead, he put on the jacket and mask, and the two left the closet after the older man had looked both ways that the coast was clear.

Soon, they were downstairs and exiting the

lobby. They approached a beat-up Volkswagen Jetta, the rear bumper missing and emerald green paint faded in patches over the body. "You'll have to drive," the man said.

"You drove here in that?"

"I came from the apartment, had to hot wire this thing from a neighbor on the other side."

"Wait." Nate stopped walking toward the vehicle. "I don't know anything about hot wiring a car."

His older self smiled. "Yeah, I learned a couple of things at the Heights."

Nate thought of the catastrophe of being stopped in a hot car without a license. "We're not taking that," Nate said. "I have Cheryl's car."

The man nodded and smiled. "Of course. Even better! We'll leave this here." He pulled on the edge of purple rubber gloves in his jeans pocket. "Got these from your kitchen and wore them in the car, so no fingerprints. Didn't want to implicate us when the cops find this."

Nate shook his head, trying not to think too hard about who he was talking to. "This way," he said and began walking to where he parked. They reached Cheryl's Malibu and Nate stopped at the rear. "I don't have a license. Do you?"

The man looked at the car, took off his mask, and

then closed his eyes and began counting backward and rubbing his hands together.

Nate winced at the scarred side of the man's face, considered a moment asking him about it, but then shook the idea away. Instead, he asked, "What are you doing?"

The older man opened his eyes. "Keeping myself in this present moment. Yes, I have a license. No, I can't drive this car." He turned to look at Nate. "Do you want me disappearing at forty miles per hour on the road?"

Nate understood his point and got into the driver's side. The man got in on the passenger side, his eyes glazed as he started counting backward again.

"Why do you do that?"

The man looked at Nate. "If I start thinking about where I've come from or thinking too much on where I may be going, I will pull myself back. Like I did the first time we met."

Nate started the engine and pulled out of the hospital parking lot. "Where are we going?"

"Turn left up ahead," the man said.

"So, what do you mean about thinking too much?" Nate turned on a green arrow at the intersection.

"You know how when you are asleep and

dreaming, and you know you are dreaming? It's quite a trip. Right? But then you think about it too much and wake yourself up."

"So, you're asleep?"

The man pointed out the windshield. "Turn right at Jerome Street. No, not asleep. I'm really here, with you. What happens to me here will follow me back. Just like you experienced this morning."

Nate thought about his feet, which were itching more than stinging now, but still reminded him of running along the rocky dirt in his socks. He turned at the intersection and continued down Jerome. "Okay, but you need to, what, concentrate to stay?"

"Something like that. If my mind is not present in each moment, not consistently aware of where I am and what I am doing, I can send myself back before I'm ready."

Nate considered what had happened to himself earlier. He was thinking about being in the past, how he saw his past self and Cheryl, and suddenly he was back in his apartment, falling out of his desk chair, where he had started. "I think I see what you mean."

"So, I've come up with tricks to keep me grounded in the past. But even when I keep this deep focus of each moment, I end up going back after an hour or so. Which is why we have to hurry. Turn right again at Spencer."

Nate knew his older self was directing him back to the apartment by a different route. As they reached the corner of Spencer and Higley, he realized why.

"Turn in here," the older man directed.

Nate parked in front of the Second Chance Pawn Shoppe, its hoity-toity spelling humbled by the dying neon flickers of the first P. He turned off the engine.

The older man leaned toward to Nate, his hands reaching into an inside pocket of the leather jacket Nate was wearing.

Nate squirmed. "Hey, what are you doing?"

"Relax, Jack." The man pulled out a white envelope from the pocket. "Stay here," he said as he got out of the car. He went inside the pawnshop, and Nate watched through the bars of the large bay windows as he approached the counter and began talking to a man who worked there.

Nate sweated in the still air of the car, the jacket he wore too warm for the late morning sun. He took it off, a badge shimmering from where it was pinned to the left side. His fingers gripped its pointed plastic edges, the word "Sheriff" embedded in Old West script.

"Jesus." Nate scoffed. He unpinned the toy badge from the jacket and threw it into the back seat.

Feeling hungry and restless, he got out of the car and locked it before going inside the shop.

Bells jangled as he walked inside. His older self leaned in toward the shop owner, a man in his early sixties with deep lines in his face that created a perpetual frown. He stood up straight and looked warily with steel-blue eyes at Nate. Nate's older self turned around, gritting his teeth.

"I thought I told you to wait in the car," he scolded.

Nate shrugged his shoulders and walked over to a glass cabinet, his older self's voice muttering, "Damn kids," as the shop owner nodded with a deep, humorless laugh.

The only other people in the shop were a young couple gazing at a jewelry case, whispering to each other. Nate ignored them, looking at the case across from them with shelves of old watches, wood-encased chess timers, and an assortment of antique clocks. He eyed a bell jar clock that resembled his mother's, but it lacked the eloquent charm of that destroyed keepsake. *I'll fix it,* he thought and then looked over at the counter where the man and shop owner continued their whispered conversation. His older self was pushing the envelope of cash across the counter as they talked, the shop owner nodding and, without looking at it, using a swift movement of his fingers to pull it to the other side of the counter where it fell out of sight. He bent over as if to pick it up, instead pulling up a shoe box up and placing it on the counter. Their conversation didn't falter, the movements quick and outside their attention. Nate's older self took the box under his arm and continued talking to the owner.

Nate spotted a rack of snack foods near the cash register and walked over, pulling off a couple of beef jerky packages and throwing them on the counter. "Buy me these, Pops, I'm starving," he said.

His older self gave him a scornful look.

"Please."

Both men straightened up. The shop owner's eyes narrowed, but his older self sighed, smiling stiffly as he pulled out his wallet and threw down a couple of bills.

"Thanks," Nate said, taking the jerky packages. The register rang as he headed toward the door. He heard his older self mumble something to the shop owner before following Nate outside.

"I forgot what a prick I was in my youth," the man said.

"Just in your youth?" Nate unlocked the car doors and then ripped open a package of jerky to stuff a piece in his mouth. He got in the car behind the wheel.

His older self sat shotgun, putting the shoe box on the floor at his feet. "I'm trying to protect you, dude," he said, putting on his seatbelt. "He's a bit trigger-happy with a twelve-gauge under the counter. Next month he'll use it on a couple of teens making off with some smart watches he had out on display."

Nate, remembering he had no license to drive, slowed down and swallowed. "How do you know that?"

"I met him at the Heights."

"I thought you said you just changed things, so you never went there."

"Sure," he said. "But I still remember it."

Nate drove in silence. His passenger started his counting exercise again, his hands tapping on the dashboard. This annoyed Nate, but he let it go. In a couple of minutes, he turned the car into Westcourt Apartments and parked in front of his door.

Inside his apartment, the older Nate looked at the modified laptop and smiled. "Quite ingenious how you scrapped that together." He sat at the desk chair, placing the shoe box on the floor near his feet. "I never made one at your age." Light from the desk lamp shone against the pinkish-purple scars on his left face.

Nate sat on the bed and ate more jerky, speaking

through his full mouth. "I thought you were me in thirty-whatever years." He paused, absorbing how oddly comfortable he had become with the concept. "How could you not have made the one I just made?"

His older self leaned back in the chair, stretching his legs. "Well, that's just the thing, Natey boy. I *do* remember. But it is a new memory. Like this conversation, or going to the pawn shop, it all is stuff I start to remember from when I was you, only a bit later. It all gets mixed in with my own memories as who I am now. It is like my history is rewriting as we talk. Understand?"

"Not really," Nate said, handing he jerky to his older self.

He shook his head. "None for me, it'll just leave a mess when I go back."

Nate paused, about to ask what he meant, but then chose not to ask. He leaned back and put the jerky package down. "So, what happened with my shoes?"

His older self tilted his head. "What do you mean?"

"When I went back—if that's what you call it—earlier today… you remember doing that. Don't you? When you were me? Well, I had shoes on, but when I went back I…"

"Socks." The man nodded with a stiff chuckle. "It

was the socks. To bring something back with you in time, you have to be touching it, physically in contact with your skin. Otherwise, it doesn't go with you."

Just then, Nate noticed his visitor's outstretched legs revealed he had no socks on under his shoes. "Oh."

"Yup. I had to hold everything to bring it here, the money in one hand, my other hand on my jacket. Kind of a pain, but it is necessary. Just some part has to have skin contact. Weird, I know."

Nate eyed the shoe box at the man's feet. "You taking that back with you, then? What is it?"

The man leaned forward. "We can't take anything back with us. That is important to remember." He tapped the box with his foot. "This is for you. But later. First, I want to make it clear that we can be hurt in the past, as I remember my feet were rather sore after that first excursion. Right?"

Nate nodded, mustering the courage to ask the question he had put off long enough. "What happened…" He pointed to his own face, circling his finger around his left cheek and eye.

The man's expression didn't change, but his eyes pierced into Nate's. "Like I said, we can bring injuries back with us."

Nate squirmed. "How did you…"

"It is part of what I came to tell you," the man said.

The older man closed his eyes a moment, his fingers against the arms of the desk chair, his lips moving as he silently counted. After a minute, he opened his eyes.

"This," he said, motioning around Nate's studio. "This is new history. It wasn't the past I lived. That past is what I want to tell you about. It starts with that fucking... that..."

"The car accident," Nate said. Nothing else would cause the man to stumble.

He nodded. "It didn't turn out the way you remember. Oh, I remember it like you do, but I also remember something different. You... we... don't remember being pulled from the car. Just waking up after it was in flames, Aunt Peggy running across the street to get to us, crying. And those screams. Mom's..." His voice broke, and he paused.

Nate looked down at his hands. He twisted his fingers together and yanked them apart, as if to pull the memory away. He took a deep breath and waited for the man to continue.

"I'm going to propose something to you." The

man leaned forward so Nate could feel his breath as he spoke. "Suppose we had a different life? Imagine, for a moment, that Mom didn't die in that accident? That even Mrs. McVey survived. Aunt Peggy. And you, of course. Think of it. What if the tragedy of our life never rolled over us the way you remember? Mom lived. Dan... *Dad*... never fell to his demons. You never fell to yours. Peggy went back to Chicago and became a successful professor and twenty years later wrote some really weird books on metaphysics that became best sellers. Cheryl started her own business and married some guy I didn't like much, but he was good for her and made her happy, so we got along well enough. She had two kids, a boy and a girl, just like her and me... you. And I... you... married Ellie." He paused, closing his eyes again and tapping the chair arms.

For a moment, Nate thought the man's features became less distinct, like a soft focus camera effect. He blinked, thinking it could be eyestrain, but the man still looked indistinct. After a few seconds, his features regained clarity.

"It was good, that life," the man continued with a wistful smile. "Really good. Except for one thing, one bit of tragedy we accepted, but was a burdensome imperfection in an otherwise excellent life."

His smile faded, and he looked down at his

hands. "Mom was injured in that accident. Her legs severely burned. I mean, deep burns that kept her in a wheelchair the rest of her life. Painful burns that she never fully recovered from." He looked back at Nate. "You know Mom, she was a trooper, always positive and forward-thinking. But I could see it in her eyes. The pain. Longing to walk again. Longing to be whole. Cheryl saw it, too. And even Dad. Aunt Peggy used a lot of the money she earned from her research and books to pay for Mom's ongoing treatment. She gained a lot of weight over the years in that wheelchair, and the skin didn't stretch properly, so she had to have surgery to expand it, so her own legs didn't cut off blood flow." The man wiped his nose against his shirt sleeve, sniffed, and then continued. "Long story short, she died when she was fifty-seven. Pretty damned young for a woman who had so much life in her. But we accepted it and life went on.

"Until, that is, Aunt Peggy died. She died at eighty-one, twenty years after Mom. She had lived a good life and left us all a tidy sum of inheritance. She also entrusted Cheryl her journal, something Cheryl shared with me. This crazy story that Aunt Peggy was the one who saved my life when I was a child. Her whole time travel story, just like the one you read. She claimed I died in that car accident, the only casualty. Even Mom escaped with just minor injury. But Aunt Peggy forgot me in that back seat, and Mom never forgave her. For that matter, she never forgave herself. So, when she was fifty-three, just like you read, she learned a technique to travel back in time and built her jabberwock.

"Something she didn't expect happened. When she traveled back in time to the day of the crash, she ran to the car and opened the door to pull me... you... out of the back seat. But this action of hers caused another difference. Maybe it was the influx of oxygen to the car when she opened that door, maybe it was everyone distracted by a strange woman entering the car, causing just enough of a pause that they didn't get out as quickly as before. But the flames got worse before Mom could escape, and she was severely injured.

"So, I got to thinking. If someone had been there to help Mom out of the car sooner, maybe she would have been spared the injuries she suffered. Maybe she could have had that life she deserved."

"Like you, I read Peggy's specifications in that journal and figured out what they were. I realized I could build this machine and fix what she didn't. Actually, fix what she *caused*."

Nate's older self sat back in the chair and looked up at the ceiling as if looking for the words he would say next. His lips moved, but he wasn't counting like before. His mouth frowned as if he had eaten something foul.

He looked back at Nate. "So, I did it. I went back. It was... the scariest fucking thing I ever did. I stood in the park, near the intersection, and saw the crash as it happened. Those flames were *huge.* But I ran to them, pushing past other bystanders to get to the front passenger door. I threw it open and the heat... oh, God, the heat! But I pulled on Mom with one hand, lifting the shattered windshield with the other, and then... and then..."

He hit the top of Nate's desk with his fist. The laptop and desk lamp shuddered from the blow. The older man remained still and then turned with a sickly smile and waved his arms, like a magician revealing his climatic prestige. "*This* is the result, Natey boy. I created this nightmare." He pointed at Nate. "I created *your life*." He licked his lips and sat back in the chair, his gaze never leaving Nate. "And I'm going to tell you how to fix it."

11

Nate felt lightheaded, the information overwhelming as he tried to absorb what he was being told. A life where Mom lived? Dad not a drunk? Growing up with two responsible parents instead of an overwhelmed aunt? These were dreams Nate put to rest long ago. And Cheryl, instead of in the hospital on life support after a lifetime of looking after Dad and him, she got married and was living a full, happy life? Even he, himself, married and unburdened by addiction? The idea made Nate swoon.

"What can I do?" he asked.

"First," his older self said, "I'll tell you what went wrong. Why our life is such a fucking disaster. It comes down to a single name: *Rico*. Rico fucking McVey."

Nate's eyes widened. Sure, Rico was responsible for what happened to Cheryl, and Nate planned to take care of that. But Rico lost his mother in the accident, too. He suffered *more* than Nate, a fact he sometimes made clear, with the deep burn injuries he still suffered from, like his near-useless left hand and scarred torso.

"Yeah," his older self said. "I see that look. 'Poor Rico.'" His mouth sneered. "Well, fuck Rico. I'll tell you what he did. When I went back in time, when I witnessed the accident and saw the flames from that gas tanker growing toward the car, I rushed to the passenger door, threw it open, reached in to pull Mom out. And what happened? Rico! That fucking boy crawled over Mom to get out first, pinning her in her seat."

The older man made fists and hit his knees, his voice changing to a higher timbre. "The flames leaped from under the dashboard and Mom is screaming and Rico... yeah, he is burning, too, but I try to push him back, get him off Mom. But Lois... Mrs. McVey... she's pushing him toward me to get him out on my side. It felt like an endless tug of war, and Rico won't move, so I pull on the fucking boy's arm, pulling him toward me to get him off Mom, pulling him out of the car. And then it exploded! Mom and Lois screaming inside. The heat... and I'm on fire now, too, and running to the park, rolling in the grass to get it out, hearing Mom's shrieks from the blazing car... and then I'm back here, poor and drunk and alone. No Ellie. No Mom. No Cheryl. No Dad." He pointed at his scarred face. "And this for my trouble. The burns came back with me, fresh and red, and I had to call for an ambulance. I made some story up about a lithium battery blowing up in my face, even though I had no evidence for that. Not that it mattered. I got treated and then sent back home to my own care. Alone and trying to figure out how *everything* went so wrong."

The man wiped his eyes with his shirt sleeve, sniffing, his face glistening with sweat. "Well, it was Rico. What he did to Cheryl is just one more thing to add to his stain on my life. Our life. She'll live for another six years, unable to talk, to communicate, her mind gone, everything she was gone. Then she'll die, and you know what? I was relieved when it happened. Relieved not because her suffering was over but because I didn't have to think about it anymore. Didn't have to visit her in that state hellhole where she was being kept alive... that living death..."

"Stop," Nate said, raising his hands. "Don't tell me all that!" He swallowed, shaking his head. "I already have a plan to stop him from hurting her."

The man let out a humorless laugh. "It won't be enough, kid. You need to go back further than that to fix what he's done."

"What do you mean?"

"It's more than just Cheryl. Think of Mom. Of Dad. Even Peggy. Rico was supposed to *die* in that car accident. Aunt Peggy went back in time to save me, and when she did, Rico died instead and everyone was happier for it. We all *thrived*. And what happened when I tried to make it perfect, so Mom could live her full life, too? Rico destroyed it. Nine-year-old Rico destroyed it for all of us."

Nate bit his lower lip. "I don't like where this is going…"

"You're getting it, then." He leaned in close to Nate, his breath hot on his face. "Patrick 'Rico' McVey must die. He must die when as a child."

Nate jumped up from where he was sitting, nearly knocking over his older self. He shook his head, pacing toward the kitchen and back. After a few moments, he stopped and stood over the older man. "Why do you need me? Why are you even telling me any of this? Go fix it yourself."

The man shook his head. "I tried. I really did. I couldn't make it back to that same moment. I could go a few days before or a few days after, but never the moment where it mattered most. I almost gave up, but I kept researching what I could do. Stayed here, in this apartment, year after year, living off government handouts and the laptops I could sell, looking for how I could fix this life, make it back to what I remembered it could be."

Nate sat back down on the bed. "Do you mean I can't even go back to yesterday? To fix what happened to Cheryl?"

"Yep. That program you devised has limitations. Just like mine did."

Nate leaned forward, holding his hands over his face. "No, no, that can't be true. I was right there. I could have... oh, shit, I could have..."

The older man put his hands on Nate's shoulders. "Feels pretty shitty. Doesn't it? I know. I know. What would you give for the opportunity to fix things?"

Nate didn't want the man to see that his eyes were wet, so he kept his head bowed. It seemed impossible that his hopes of a few hours ago were another mistake in his life of mistakes.

"I can't believe there's nothing..." Then he felt his face grow warm, an electrifying jolt in his chest. He looked up, scowling. "Man, why did you come here just to tell me that? You said I could fix it!"

"That's it!" He patted Nate on the shoulders and then sat back in the chair. "That's the fury that you need to get it done. Yes, you *can* still fix it."

"How?"

"I spent years researching. I won't go into the dead-ends and setbacks, but it was all there already in Peggy's journal. I just didn't see it, and when I did, I started experimenting. And finally, I got it!"

"What was it? Tell me, man." Nate fidgeted with impatience.

"Peggy used MIDI format for the musical notes. But MIDI has a lot more going in it than just notes. It's designed for synth, to compose detailed music for each instrument, including reverb and velocity, the time each note plays and how loud or soft it plays. That was the solution! It made a huge difference. I could fine-tune the tones she established, conveying them in specific velocity and that allowed me to pick a time to return to, within seconds of the moment I wanted."

Nate sat up straight. "You enhanced the program?"

"Yes! It isn't perfect, but now it will get you just seconds to where you want to go." He pulled up his shirt sleeve and pulled out a flash drive he had attached to his wrist under his watchband. "This is our ticket." He plugged it into Nate's laptop and powered up the device.

"Wait," Nate said. "Why are you giving this to me?

If you fixed the problem, you can just do this yourself."

The man sighed. "It took me years to figure this out. That's why. And I have a law of time travel for you. Besides only going back to a time and place we were present in the past, we have a limit to how far we can go back. I estimate it is only about seventy percent of our life that we can travel back. I'm fifty-six and at this age can only manage to go back to when I was around sixteen, after everything was already the shits. I don't know why this is, but believe me, I've tried to get past this limitation. It never works. Sure, I could take Rico out when he was in high school, but all things considered, that wouldn't do much. Mom would still be gone, Dad a drunk, on and on and on." He logged in to the computer with his fingerprint and copied a file from the flash drive to the laptop. "There, it's ready."

"I... I can't do this, man." Nate stood up and paced back to his kitchen.

His other self stood up and followed him. "Yes, you can. You have to."

Nate turned to the man. "I... I don't even have a weapon."

The older man opened his mouth to say something just as his watch began beeping. "Another law of time travel: We only get a couple of hours per trip. Don't ask me why." He placed both hands on Nate's shoulders. "Don't worry, the program I put on the computer won't leave with me. It's a copy and now exists here, in this time stream. You have to do this so everything will be as it should be again. You *must* kill Rico McVey. Kill him before he brings disaster to our life…"

The man diffused and vanished. Nate stumbled back, blinking, from the sudden absence of hands on his shoulders. Something fell to the floor with a soft thud. Two purple gloves from Nate's kitchen, the ones the man had taken that were still in his pocket.

Nate ignored them and walked over to his laptop. The flash drive was gone, but the copied program remained in the folder the man had loaded it to. His foot tapped against the box by his desk chair, the shoe box the man had picked up from the pawnshop. He picked it up and, pulling off the lid, set it on the bed.

Inside the box lay a black Glock 9mm handgun. Two cartridges lay next to it, each filled with fifteen rounds.

12

Nate put the lid back on the box and pushed it under his desk. He had a gun just like it until Cheryl took it away months earlier, when she feared he might be drunkenly careless with it. He also suspected she thought he was suicidal, worried that he would become impatient with his efforts to drink himself to a slow death. He let her take it since she had a point about the careless part. Suicidal? He didn't drink to kill himself; he drank to escape the life handed to him. In a small, deep place, he hoped he might emerge from a night of blurred abandon into a life worth living. Something Cheryl would have told him was magical thinking.

His phone buzzed in his back pocket, and he pulled it out. Dad again. He cringed as he swiped to accept the call.

"Hey."

"What happened to you?" His father's voice sounded desperate. "Rico said you were here and some man from security dragged you…"

"I'm at home, Dad," Nate said, "but what the hell was Rico doing there? You know he is responsible for what happened."

"Nate." His father sighed. "I thought you had been arrested."

"Jesus, no." Nate rubbed his eyes with the fingers of his free hand. "I went home, or I would have broken that asshole's jaw."

Silence for a moment and then his father said, "I remember when you boys were best friends."

Nate shook his head to clear his mind. "How's Cheryl?"

Silence again. Nate heard the rustle of the phone against fabric and then the static of Dan's breath. "She's… I think you should be here, Nate."

Nate straightened. "Tell me what's happening."

"The doctors… I wish you didn't make me tell you this on the phone, but the doctors said we need to prepare ourselves."

"Is she worse?" Nate's fingers trembled, and he tightened his grip on the phone.

"Well, they aren't confident she's going to get much better, and what they are saying is…" He cleared his throat. "They're saying I might need to decide soon if we want to continue... uh, continue her life support."

"No, Dad!" Nate stood up and paced the room. "Don't you dare do that! I'll... I'll... as long as she has a chance, don't do that!"

"That's just the point, Nate." His father sounded resigned and old as he spoke. "Her chances are getting worse, her time with us might..." He cleared his throat again and inhaled. "Can you come back? Rico's gone home and we should both be sitting with her."

"Okay, on my way." Nate ended the call without waiting for his father's response.

Fucking Rico. He *should* kill the bastard. Get the Glock and find him and shoot him in his fucking head. No time travel necessary.

But that wouldn't change anything for Cheryl. That wouldn't fix this nightmare life.

Nate sat at his desk chair, the laptop open with the spindled lights jutting out from the sides and the screen dark. He tapped on the fingerprint sensor and the screen lit up. The program his visitor had left him was named "PeiPei_5.7.0.1." This, Nate knew, wasn't magical thinking. This was his real chance to make things right.

He picked up the gun from the shoe box, feeling

its weight in his hand. Hold it, go back in time, and shoot Rico. But as a child? Would he even consider such a thing if Rico hadn't hurt Cheryl, if his violent arrogance hadn't started this whole thing? Two days ago, would it have even crossed his mind that Rico was the common factor for the misery in his life?

Nate could write a list of those influences that lead him into his personal hell, and his father would be at the top of it. Not Rico. Not even close. Until last night, he wouldn't be on the list at all. They were friends in middle school and high school and then drinking buddies. Rico pressured his father, Geoffrey McVey, to get Nate a job at their company, McVey Land and Living.

Yes, a series of late attendance, sick days, and general failure to finish projects got him fired, and a lot of that was because of his frequent long nights at the bars with Rico, who couldn't get fired because he also worked for his father's company. To be fair, Rico could handle his liquor, and he knew when to stop drinking and just flirt with the girls who usually politely ignored him (if they were nice) or openly grimaced (if they were rude, which was more often than not) after seeing his withered hand or the scars peeking out from his shirt collar.

Rico would cover the pain in his face with stupid jokes and act like he didn't care, but Nate knew he did. Which was why it was so great when Cheryl got back from college and actually dated him for almost a year. Living across the street, they all grew up together, and she knew what she was getting into. After two boyfriends cheated on her, Rico's familiarity was a bonus and helped her to overlook some of the less admirable qualities of his personality.

He had, she told Nate, a real deep and caring persona, if you could get past his surface bullshit, the mask he put on to hide his grief from rejection he often got because of his prominent scars. But even she couldn't continue the relationship when his controlling jealousy and general assholeness got in the way.

Nate unplugged the laptop so he could insert the lights for the left side. He couldn't kill Rico as a child. It was way too extreme. This life Nate had he could live with, at least until the night before. Fix that, reverse the nightmare of the past twenty-four hours, and he would have Cheryl back and a whole new attitude toward his life, knowing now that as bad as things might seem, they could always get far, far worse. This experience put things into perspective. He would start fresh with Alcoholics Anonymous. He'd put his own house in order, as they said. And no kid had to die. He just needed to fix what happened the night before.

Nate considered what he would do. He fumbled through his dresser's sock drawer and pulled out an old red and blue pullover ski mask, a gift from Dad years ago that he hated to use because it made him look like a funky Spider-Man. He loaded a clip to the gun before picking up his laptop and heading to the bathroom. Closing the door, he sat on the edge of the bathtub with the laptop on his knees and gripped the gun in his right hand, the ski mask in the other. Then he remembered to take off his socks. He'd want his shoes this time.

He clicked on the icon, and the jabberwock began to flash and sing its tones. Nate breathed in and out, staring into the multicolored lights that danced before his eyes and at the sides of his head. The chords struck, and the warm vibration down his spine crawled over him like living fingers, a stronger response than he'd experienced before. The room darkened, his body weightless as the dancing lights seemed to disengage from the front screen and side spindles to dance around him like multicolored fireflies.

Whatever was happening, it was stronger with the enhanced program. Nate sucked in air and concentrated, gripping the gun and ski mask with his hands to feel their contrasting weight and texture. He felt like he did the night before, being in his studio on the floor, that moment of intense peace he felt just before Cheryl arrived. That moment, just before everything that worked in his life fell apart. The lights lifted him on a wave of music, higher and higher…

Late afternoon light dances through the shadows of a tree on the ceiling, white and orange ripples like waves of water. Nate's head is against something hard. He blinks. He is on his back looking up. He squiggles his numb body to move on his side, but his legs drape over the side of the bathtub, where he has fallen backward into the basin. Feeling creeps over his skin like cold sand pouring over him, and he senses soft knitted fabric in one hand, hard metal in the other.

Nate scrambles to sit up and remembers what he had been doing. He looks around, the laptop nowhere to be seen. *Did it work?* Nate holds his breath, sitting himself on the edge of the tub and looking at the door. The main room on the other side is quiet, but he resists the urge to open the door and look.

Several minutes pass. He feels the hyperawareness of his surroundings that he experienced before. He knows he has traveled *somewhere* (or some time?), but whether he reached his intended destination, he cannot be certain until he opens the door. Nate concentrates on the grain of the wood, the brass-plated knob stripped of its shine from years of use by various tenants. He turns his head with a slight tilt to the left, his ear to the door. The silence from the other side could mean the studio is empty. It might mean he has over or under-shot his intended moment in time.

The room has darkened since his arrival. Sunset. So, that would fit his intended time. It is warm and humid in the small room, his forehead growing damp with perspiration. His knees ache as he leans forward, and his impatience grows with the pain.

Open the door, Natey boy. See where you landed.

His older self's voice taunts his thoughts, egging him into motion. He stands up, moving his feet so he stands against the door, so close he can smell the wood and old paint with a hint of mildew. He places the ski mask under his arm and places his freed hand around the knob, cool and smooth. He grips it, feeling it slowly turn in his grip, the click of its latch retracting. Just a peek… just a…

Nate hears the unmistakable squeak of

bedsprings and freezes. He releases the doorknob with a slow, quiet movement. More sounds, a zipper being pulled and then the clinking of metal against metal, a sloshing of ice followed by the crack of a can being popped open.

Nate steps away from the door, his back straight. If he is right, in just a moment he will hear a pounding on the door. Nate's hands tremble. This could be it. This could be the moment that fixes everything.

Pound, pound, pound!

Nate jerks at the sound, his sweaty hand losing its grip on the gun as he fumbles with it. He falls to his knees to keep it in his lap, held against his leg with his hand, before it can clatter to the floor. He breathes in slowly, ignoring the tickle of sweat down his face.

"Nate! Open the door. Nate!" *Cheryl.*

The sound of her voice tightens his throat, a lump of grief and potential relief that torments him. It is almost his cue to action.

Nate controls his breathing, feeling himself losing a layer of the hyperawareness and then another, a sensation of drifting away. *No! I must stay.* He places his hand against the door, the smooth grain of the wood against his fingers. He remembers his older self's routine and begins counting backward from ten. He feels his surroundings harden, become sharp again in his mind and senses. He's here. He is present in this moment. He is almost ready.

The voices on the other side of the door rise in argument. "Get some balls, man." Rico, snide and nasty. "Maybe she can pick them out for you."

Anger unfurls in Nate, and he is grateful for it. He needs the energy of it to do what he must do. He pulls the ski mask over his head and tightens his grip on the gun. He turns the doorknob and pulls open the door with a sharp movement.

It swings into his feet, the rebound unsettling Nate's balance, and he falls into the door. Nate stumbles forward as the door swings closed from his weight, controlling the movement enough to prevent it from slamming shut.

Shit! Nate's breath hisses between clenched teeth and tight lips. *Stupid, stupid, stupid!*

He listens for any sign that those in the main room have heard him.

"*I didn't invite you here! Go!*" Nate's own voice, raging at Cheryl on the other side of the door.

In spite of his shame hearing the harsh words, Nate exhales a brief sigh of relief. His clumsy attempt at entering the room didn't attract attention. But he still has mere seconds to make his entrance to prevent what is about to happen. He steps to the side of the door so it will clear his feet while swinging inward.

Nate turns the knob and then inhales a sharp, deep breath. He pulls the door open and then bounds into the room. With the gun in both hands, he aims at the trio near the front door. "Hey!" He deepens his voice, the shout echoing against the walls.

The three are startled, jumping as they turn to look at Nate. Cheryl yelps. Nate's other self shouts, "What the..." Rico backs up and then freezes.

"Okay, y'all, git out of here!" Nate, to his own surprise, is using a caricature of a Southern accent to disguise his voice. The three stare at him, frozen, eyes wide. None move. "Y'all heard me! Fuckin' git out, and no one gits hurt!" He waves his gun.

Nate's other self and Cheryl remain frozen near the front door, but Rico backs toward the kitchen.

"Hey!" Nate shouts, waving the gun toward him. Rico freezes. "Fuckin' *out*! I'll just git what I came fer and then be on my way. *Move!*"

Rico moves forward, toward the front door, when Nate is hit by a heavy object slamming into his back, throwing him into the pantry door near the kitchen entrance. Glass shatters as Nate turns around. The glass dome of the clock scatters in pieces along the kitchen linoleum. Cheryl is standing at the small table where it had been, her eyes narrow with fury and fear as she breathes in deep, quick movements.

As Nate recovers himself, Rico dashes to the bed, his right hand dipping into the front pocket of the blue cooler. Nate tries aiming his gun toward him, but Rico is quick and pulls out his own Smith & Wesson handgun, moving to hold it toward Nate with his withered left hand supporting his right.

Before Rico can aim, Nate lunges toward him, tackling him. They both fall onto the bed. Nate struggles to remain on top of him, his right hand holding on to Rico's wrist to keep him from aiming the gun at him. Rico pushes against Nate, trying to roll over as Nate jams his knees into Rico's abdomen, pinning him as the mattress shifts under their weight. Grunting, Nate loses his balance as Rico squirms under him, his right hand's knuckles white as he grips the gun. Nate pushes Rico's arm upward and Rico fires into the ceiling. Nate jerks back from the blast, his ears buzzing as bits of plaster rain down. Rico, recovering from the recoil, struggles to maintain a grip on his gun as Nate lunges forward, slamming Rico's arm against the back wall, and the gun falls free, clattering behind the bed. His advantage restored, Nate rolls off the bed and stands with his gun, preparing to aim it again.

Arms grab around Nate's waist, and he falls sideways and hits the carpeted floor. Cheryl grabs his wrists, and Nate struggles to get back control. He pulls one arm free of her grip, but she still has her fingers around the wrist of his hand holding the gun. With her other hand, she grabs at his face, her fingers reaching for his eyes. Nate turns his head away as her hands grip at the ski mask, pulling it off his head as he struggles to get control of his gun. She holds the knitted mask, her mouth dropping open as her widening eyes look into his face.

Arms wrap around Nate's chest and neck, pain crackling down his throat and spine as he is pulled backward. He jerks and twists from the surprise movement, the gun in his hand discharging with a piercing crack. His fingers stinging from the jolt, Nate lowers his gun, the acrid smell of burning gunpowder assaulting his nose as he jerks his elbows into the person holding him, and the grip loosens.

Nate turns around, blinking as he looks into his own face. His other self stares in shock and disbelief. His lips part in a silent gasp, as if trying to form words. Instead, he emits a wailing cry.

"*Cheryl!*"

He hasn't even looked at Nate, but over his

shoulder, and pushes him away as he rushes around him. Nate turns, his eyes following his other self rushing to Cheryl. She is standing against the pantry door, her hands gripping just below her chest, a crimson blossom of blood spilling between her fingers. Her knees buckle as she slides down, her eyes glassy and unseeing.

Nate screams. The lights in the room flash as an assault of new memories flow to his mind. *Cheryl shot by the intruder... her sightless gaze as her body becomes still in his arms, blood on his shirt, on his jeans, on his hands...*

Nate stands up and runs. He runs out the front door, past the gathering neighbors, through the parking lot and toward the street. He crosses the avenue without looking, the screech of tires and honks of horns blaring past him, unnoticed. He makes it across, running into a dark field of weeds and dirt as more new memories flooded his mind. *The intruder running away... the neighbors standing dumbly by, no one stopping him... Rico bawling and running away instead of calling for help... the ambulance miraculously arriving... the police questioning him... the silent ambulance, a stretcher being lifted inside, a dark, covered form on top... the cops finding Rico's gun...*

The sun falls behind the mountains as he runs,

the world around him dissembling in the deepening twilight...

Nate thrashed against the bathroom walls, dropping the gun and ski mask. His laptop fell to the floor, the spindles breaking loose from the sides. He kicked the laptop and then picked it up and threw it into the bathtub, grunting and swearing as he smashed the screen with his toes and crushed the keyboard with his heels. He turned and threw open the bathroom door, the gun spinning against the tile and hitting the wall. He picked it up, took it with him to the main room, and threw it toward the bookshelves. It hit the wall and fell somewhere behind his desk.

She's dead. The realization struck him like a bolt of lightning. *She's dead and nothing can be done.* And the darkening truth of these new memories grew far worse than Nate's secret knowledge that the intruder only fired at Cheryl because Nate grabbed him from behind. He could not escape the damning guilt of it: *I was also the intruder.*

His previous memories made no difference. Those events didn't exist anymore. Her injury, her helpless form hooked to tubes and machines in the hospital bed, his hope of restoring her so none of it happened... all still real in his mind, but nonexistent in this altered life. She was dead. She was dead because he fired the shot that killed her.

He turned to the pantry, its door splintered with a hole from the bullet and dusted with grayish-green powder from the cops looking for fingerprints. Below it, on the carpet, a circular stain of dried blood where Cheryl had died in his arms. Nate sat on the bed, his face in his hands, and cried.

13

An hour later, as the despairing numbness settled over him, Nate examined the wreckage in the bathroom. What had his older self told him? That *he* had created this shit hole life? "Well, bubba," Nate mumbled into the empty room, "I just gave it my own special touch."

He half expected his older self to appear in the gloom, to bring him a new chance to fix what Nate had destroyed. Only the silence responded. Nate grabbed the rug from the floor before turning off the light and shutting the door.

He lay the rug at the base of the pantry, keeping his eyes upward to avoid viewing the reddish-brown stain he covered. In the kitchen, the broken clock's pieces still spread along the floor, where it had landed after Cheryl threw it at the intruder. At Nate. He had cleaned up a similar ruin once before, in that different, nonexistent life. Now, he would have to again. But he couldn't deal with that now.

Nate grabbed his jacket and keys. Opening the front door, he paused, his exit blocked by yellow tape with black letters: *Police Line Do Not Cross*. Nate choked back a despairing grunt as he broke through the tape.

Cheryl's car sat in the spaces in front of his apartment. On the dashboard sat his forgotten lunch. In this new life, he hadn't used the car yet. His father had picked him up, took him home to the house he grew up in, to his old bedroom, before leaving Nate by going to his own room and shutting the door. His father would probably wonder why he wasn't at the house, if he bothered to check. Nate didn't care.

As he had in that other life, Nate threw the lunch into the bushes and then started Cheryl's car with the keys she had forgotten after locking the club over the steering wheel. He might as well redo one other thing he had done before. It was time for a visit to The Stray Cat.

The first, a dark cobalt liquid, bittersweet and warm down his throat. *Cheryl's eyes...* His thoughts still stung, so he had the bartender slip him another. He barely tasted it, but the surrounding conversations faded to unintelligible chatter. *Dad's face on that ride home, his pale skin, his glistening eyes that barely glanced at Nate.*

"One of those," Nate said, pointing to a pale green concoction sipped by the man next to him at the counter. Sharp with citrus, it burned its way down. The countertop he leaned onto felt less real, the space of the room more distant. Good, good. But not good enough. *The numbing jolt of the gun in his hand... Cheryl's stare of shock and disbelief...* He took another and then another, mumbling confessions to himself as pink and blue neon flickered from the window beside him.

Footsteps pattered on the carpet beside him. Nate lay flat on his stomach, the mattress seeming to bob and twist like a small boat on water. A rumble of movement near the bookshelf as his mind floated to awareness. A crackle of plastic followed by the creak of someone sitting down in the desk chair.

"Wake up."

Nate shifted on the bed. "Sheeping…" Hadn't this happened before? *Oh, wow,* he thought, *déjà vu.*

"Come on, man, wake up." A hand on his back, shaking him.

He's back. Nate smiled to himself. *He'll show me how to fix it, like the last time.* He stretched, flickering his eyes open to adjust to the stinging light. The man sat on his desk chair, a silhouette against the desk lamp. In his hand, the figure held something. Nate's slowly opening eyes adjusted to the glare, and the features of his guest materialized to clarity. A plaid, long-sleeved shirt. Curly dark hair. A goatee.

Rico.

Nate sat up on his elbows. "Wha…" he blinked his eyes. "What are you doing here, man?"

Rico sighed. "I thought the same thing of you. This is still a crime scene, you know." He shook the object in his hand, a clear plastic bag with something heavy inside it.

A gun. *The* gun.

Nate sat up and swung his legs over the edge of the bed. He was still fully dressed, his jeans stained on his thigh, perhaps a spilled drink or maybe puke. It was still damp.

"What is this, man?" he said, rubbing the spot on

his leg. A mixture of memories flooded his muddled mind, igniting fury and despair: Rico pushing Cheryl so she knocked her head, but that wasn't right. No, Rico didn't do that. Rico pulled a gun. Messed up Nate's simple plan to get him outside, away from Cheryl.

"I don't…" Rico leaned forward and then back, gripping the bag with the gun in his right hand. Moisture glistened from his swollen eye. "How did you do it?" He cleared his throat. "I mean, *why* did you do it?"

Nate's mind cleared as he stared at the gun. "I didn't do it, man. You saw it, some asshole came in here and…"

"It was *you!*" Rico shouted. "I don't know how you did it. I can't make any sense of it…" He combed through his hair with his withered left hand, shaking his head. "But it was you. I saw your face when she pulled off the mask, that stupid mask… I even remember when your dad gave it to you. And *you* held *this gun.*" He shook the bag. "*You* shot it at Cheryl." Rico inhaled and looked away.

Nate swayed on the bed, folding his arms around his stomach. "You saw him run away…"

"Goddammit, Nate. It was just the three of us in here the whole time."

He opened his mouth, trying to form a denial, but there it was, the gun he had held. The gun he had fired.

Rico shook his head. "I don't understand it, man. I just don't…" He straightened up. "It was lying *right there*," and he pointed to the corner by the bookshelf. "I don't know how the idiot cops missed it, but I'll be damned if I'm going to take the fall for what happened.

"Those cops don't like my family much, you know. Father tries to appease, throwing his cash around to any crooked cop who'll take a bribe. They call him Big Boy, and he's handled enough cops on the beat to keep what goes on at these properties under the radar. But since the last election, the new powers that be have been hankering to make a show of cleaning up corruption. And now the Big Boy's loser son is involved. Girl dead. Gun in his hand. And on Big Boy's property, too.

"They took the bullet from the ceiling, matches the gun. They're itching to make an arrest. *My* arrest. Father's not going to stop them. He'll let them to show he isn't complicit in any cover-up. Oh, he'll give me some help. 'I'll get you the best lawyers, *Patty*,' he said." Rico winced as he spoke the girlish version of his name. "'But I'm not bailing you out when they take you in.' Father made it clear he will let me rot in jail until the trial is over." Rico scowled and then leaned forward. "But *I didn't do this*. I didn't hurt her. I couldn't hurt her, man. I *loved* her."

Rico sniffed, wiped his nose with his shirtsleeve, and then looked at the gun. "I'm betting this gun has the bullets that match her wounds. My gun's didn't, and so far that is the only thing keeping them from carting me over to the station in cuffs. But I'm not stupid. Give them time. They'll convince a coroner that, perhaps, the wounds aren't conclusive. Father won't stand in the way. He has his own interests to protect." He sighed. "I'm not factored into that."

Rico stood up, his shoulders slouched. "I saw it was you who shot her, Nate," he said with a weary tone. "I don't know why, or how you made things look the way they did. But I'm betting everything the cops will find your prints all over this." He held the bag up.

Nate remained on the bed, frozen, staring at Rico and unable to speak. What could he say? Rico was right, and his friend knew it.

Rico pulled open the front door and scowled. "You wore a fucking mask, man, but no gloves? It's like you *wanted* to be caught." Shaking his head, he gripped the bag in his right hand and walked out. "I just don't get it, man. I don't get any of it." He closed the door with a sharp thud.

Nate sat on the bed, staring at the spot Rico had last stood. He could get up, rush him, pull the gun out of his hand. Then what? Run away? Hide the gun somewhere else? It was hopeless.

As he heard Rico's car pull away, Nate dragged himself out of the bed. He staggered, still affected by his bender a few hours earlier, and found himself standing at the bathroom door. The remains of the laptop and its light extensions were still scattered over the floor.

He could rebuild it. He just needed some time. Nate felt a surge of determination and grabbed his backpack. He picked up the laptop and broken pieces with clumsy hands, dropping some parts and crawling along the floor to grasp them again. He bumped his head against the edge of the pedestal sink and sat on the bathtub edge.

Move, he thought, rubbing the back of his scalp and waiting for the pinprick sparkles to stop zipping around in front of his eyes. He stood up, slinging the backpack over his shoulders. He would hide out somewhere. He walked to his desk and pulled open the top drawer, pulling out his wallet and any cash he had. He counted the bills, realizing he would need more cash than he had on hand. Thinking as quickly as he could, he realized he would have to see his father first. He should have been there, anyway, not drinking it up and returning to the apartment. The scene of the crime. *Stupid, Nate, stupid.*

He stuffed the cash he found into his pockets and left.

14

The car sat among the few vehicles parked at The Stray Cat, where he had left it under the glow of the amber streetlight. Nate recalled with hazy memory the bartender refusing him more drinks, Nate getting testy, and some burly guy escorting him out by the arm . The man hovered over Nate like he was a dog on a leash until an Uber to show up and take him home. The man took cash from his pockets as well. Probably more than to pay for the ride, but Nate hadn't been in a condition to protest.

Nate's shoes scraped against the lot's graveled surface as he approached the car, the sense of *déjà vu* creeping over him once again. He reached into his pockets, his hand fishing through the paper bills he stuffed into them. A spark of panic pierced him in the gut as he feared he had left the keys back at the apartment. He pulled out bills, not caring that they fell to the ground at his feet as he poked around.

"Aw, come on, give me a break," he muttered as he pulled everything out of his right front jeans pocket and threw it to the ground. A jingle of metal gave him hope as he bent down, the gleam of the keys filling him with relief and then annoyance. "Mother fuckers," he muttered as he put the key ring around his middle finger, grabbed at all the cash he spilled, and stuffed the crumpled bills back into his pocket. He could organize all of it later. For now, he needed to get his ass out of the empty lot in one of the worst areas of town.

He passed only a few cars as he drove. His head throbbed as he glanced about for any signs of a cop car. Nothing could be worse than being stopped now without a license, prior DUIs, and still in the process of sobering up from his latest bender. Nate checked to be sure he had the headlights turned on and kept his speed as close to the posted limit as he could. He'd done this enough times that the skill returned to him with a body memory like riding a bike, a skill that worked well until that night he only had his daytime running lights on and got pulled over.

He drove into the West Central neighborhood where he grew up, the familiar homes dark and silent, the windows reflecting the tawny glow of the streetlights, like winking eyes as he passed.

Nate pulled the car over a block from his father's house, parking it behind a large 4x4 truck, hoping it would obscure the car at least from one direction of traffic. If the cops started looking for Nate, they might look for Cheryl's car as well. He was clear-headed enough not to park it at his father's house like a flashing beacon stating, "Nate's here!"

He locked the doors and secured his backpack over his shoulders. Then he walked onto the long neck of Autumn Lane, the neighborhood he grew up in that ended in a cul-de-sac. His feet crunched against the leaves that littered the sidewalks, the houses behind maple and cottonwood trees dark but for the warmth of porch lights. It was after midnight, and most everyone was asleep on a midweek night.

He approached the house he grew up in at the mouth of the cul-de-sac's semicircle. The porch light was off, the front yard illuminated by the sodium glow of the streetlight standing near the old McVey house across the street. Geoffrey McVey and Rico had moved out years earlier to a high-end area with a view of the river, just after Nate and Rico graduated high school. The flickering blue glow from the front windows revealed the current occupants inside watching television, but Nate had never met them.

Nate walked up the driveway of the house he grew up in. His father's decades-old Cadillac DeVille sat in the driveway, the front fender dented, and the cherry-red paint faded in large spots on the top and hood. A plastic red jerrycan lay on its side on the concrete. Dan kept about twenty of these cans, filled them where he could find gas at the cheapest, and then used them when prices spiked. Nate and Cheryl would joke to each other that their father probably used more gas searching around the city and neighboring towns for the cheapest prices than he gained by filling the five-gallon containers, but Peggy reminded them it was a way for him to feel in control, so they rarely teased him about it.

Nate picked up the empty can. The car's fuel cover was open, and the cap dangled to the side. Nate screwed the cap in place and snapped the cover shut before approaching the house's front door. The structure stood in contrast to the surrounding homes of neatly manicured lawns and fresh paint.

The paint on the house was faded, some siding rotted around the front windows and in need of replacement, and a tangle of weeds adorned the front yard. Aunt Peggy had been on Dan's case for months to take care of the upkeep, but he refused to spend the money to hire anyone, always promising he'd get to it "soon." His projects were often started and then left incomplete, exhibited by the half-painted trim around Cheryl's bedroom window begun almost a year earlier.

Light from her bedroom glinted through the slats of the shuttered window. A shadow moved, and for one moment Nate wondered if he would go inside and she would be there, performing her yoga or studying for an exam with earbuds on and dancing in her desk chair to her favored pop tunes.

Of course, it couldn't be. It had to be his father, and Nate's stomach tightened with the dread of facing him. If he was doing in Cheryl's room what he had done with Aunt Peggy's...

Nate hurried to the front door. He still had the house keys on his own ring, but he found the door unlocked as he turned the knob. He walked inside and entered the hall to the bedrooms.

He passed Peggy's old bedroom, empty of any sign of her except for a bed and desk. Cheryl was inconsolable the day their aunt died. She begged Nate to stay, so he slept in his old bedroom for a couple of nights. During this stay, he woke to find Dan inside Peggy's room, his eyes bloodshot and weary, tossing everything of their aunt's into black, heavy-duty trash bags. Clothing, books, knickknacks, framed photos from the wall, everything. He tore through the room, swiping all her desktop's contents with his arm and pulling down LED lights she had strung up around her desk. He pulled open her desk drawers, dumping pens, paper clips, a stapler, a pair of scissors, stuffing it all into the bags.

Nate stood in the doorway, his fingers gripping the doorframe, white with fury. His father was erasing her from their lives, everything she had or had done, even that obsession of her final weeks, tossed as garbage into the bags. Cheryl stood in the hallway, sobbing at Nate to do something.

Nate ran inside the room, pulling on Dan's arms to stop him. His father's face was sweaty and red, and Nate could smell the Jim Beam venting from his body like vapor. Dan pushed Nate back and continued his assault on Peggy's possessions. When Nate tried pulling him back by the shoulders, Dan's fist punched into Nate's throat.

The room darkened as stars spun like embers from a burning stack of wood, and Nate collapsed in a heap, choking and grasping at his throat. His father took no more notice of him and continued to fill the bags with Peggy's possessions. Nate coughed and stood up, each breath he took like fire, and then staggered to sit on the bed. By now Dan was at her closet, grabbing a fresh bag, ripping her clothes off hangers and stuffing them inside with quick fury.

Nate, recovering his breath, decided then he was done with his father forever. He stood up, his hand brushing against Aunt Peggy's leather-bound book she was always writing in, her reading glasses folded on top. He grabbed the book, the reading glasses on top falling to the floor. He handed it to Cheryl, who took it with trembling hands and held it to her chest. She had seen what their father had done to him and asked no more of Nate that night. They both went to their rooms and shut their doors.

Nate shut his eyes and breathed deeply to release the memory. He needed to focus. He needed to get cash from his father so he could hide out somewhere for a while, enough time to rebuild his jabberwock.

He found his father in Cheryl's room, his back to the door as he sat at Cheryl's white desk. A bottle of whiskey, almost empty, lay on the floor near the chair. Her room appeared untouched, and Nate inhaled with relief.

Dan's shoulders trembled, and Nate felt embarrassment and guilt roll over him as he realized his father was crying. He fought the temptation to turn away and wait in his own room. He needed to get going, the sooner the better. Nate raised his hand and knocked it against the doorjamb.

His father sat up straight and turned around. His cheeks shimmered with tears, and he wiped them away as he inhaled, his expression shifting to a neutral pose. "You look awful, Nate."

The comment threw Nate. He probably did look awful. He could tell he at least smelled awful. "I..." He considered where to begin, but his mind went blank.

His father stood up, his hand on the desk to balance himself as his legs wobbled and then bent over and set the Jim Bean bottle upright. Straightening up again, he stepped toward Nate and placed a hand on his shoulder. "Clean yourself up, Nate. Then we can talk."

Nate nodded and then turned before his father could see him cry. Why the hell was he being so nice to him? So damned *fatherly*. That was a long time coming. By the time he was in the shower, his grief had shifted to anger. Did he think being so fucking nice now would make up for what he'd done or, more to the truth, *hadn't* done, over all those years?

Nate dressed in clean clothes from his closet. The gray shirt was loose, as were the jeans. He had lost weight since he last wore these clothes and tightened up the belt a couple of notches.

He grabbed his backpack—he didn't want the remains of his jabberwock to be far from him—and found his father back in Cheryl's room, sitting again at her desk. The Jim Beam bottle was gone, and his fingers caressed the frame of the same photograph Nate had at his apartment, the one of Cheryl, him, and Peggy at the local fair.

"Your sister was happy this day. All of us were."

"Dad, I need…" Again, Nate found himself at a loss for words. It felt pointless to ask this man for anything.

Dan looked over at Nate. "Tell me how this happened." His lips trembled as he spoke, and Nate feared the man would start blubbering again, but his face calmed.

"It was an accident."

Anger flashed across his father's face. "What *kind* of accident?"

"Dad…" Nate gripped his backpack, wondering if he should just turn and leave. But where would he go? "Don't make me say it, please."

His father lightly tapped his cell phone, which sat face down on top of Cheryl's desk. "Just before you showed up, Rico called. Looking for you."

Shit. "What did he say?"

Dan Johnson sighed. "Why did you have a gun, Nate? A gun?" His eyes looked bewildered. "Your sister took yours away, for your protection, because she *loved you* Nate. It's still there, in the shed, because I checked after I talked to him. But why did you get another one? What were you planning to do?"

What had Rico told him? "It wasn't my gun, Dad. Some guy broke in with a gun and Rico had his and… and…" Nate's double-memory flashed in his mind, watching the man run away past the neighbors, and him, the so-called intruder, running away past everyone, trying to escape the inescapable. "There were witnesses, Dad. They saw this guy run away, so…" He almost said, *I didn't do it*, but the lie stuck in his throat.

Nate's father looked toward a poster of Dali's *Persistence of Memory*, reworked as tabby cats with clocks on their bellies. "Why would Rico tell me…" He bowed his head, his left hand clinching to a fist as he looked up to Nate. "Did you shoot your sister?"

Nate stepped back and leaned against the doorframe. "I… what… Jesus, Dad, how can you even ask me that?" Not quite a denial he wanted to state, but as close as he could get without lying. He glanced over at the opposite wall, a poster of some dude named Harry Styles wearing a bright pink shirt and white bell-bottom pants, smiling back as if mocking Nate.

Dan frowned, his head bobbing in a slow resignation. "Where have you been? Your apartment?"

Nate felt his knees weakening. "Dad..."

"Did Rico find a gun there while you slept it all off?"

"Tell me what he told you."

His father looked up at the ceiling. "Yeah." His eyes shifted toward Nate but not quite at him, a bit to the side, as if he couldn't bear to look at his son. "Why can't you deny any of this?" A tear snaked down the side of his nose, along his left cheek. "Christ, Nate, I lost *both* my children last night. Didn't I?"

"Please, I just need some cash. I can fix this, Dad. I just need some..."

"Fix what?" Dan looked into Nate's eyes, his voice rising. "Your sister is *dead*, Nate." His face crumbled as his voice rose to a yell. "My *daughter* is dead and you think you can *fix* that?"

Nate blinked as the shutters behind his father flashed red and then blue. Cold rushed over him, his arms and legs trembling. "Dad, what did you do?"

"Turn yourself in, Nate. For once in your life, do the right thing and turn yourself in." A siren briefly whooped from the driveway, punctuating his father's comment.

A cold terror seized Nate. "Oh, god, Dad! No!" He gripped his backpack and turned, running down the hall, through the kitchen and out the back door. The chilly night air stung his arms and face, penetrating his thin shirt. His feet crunched through a tangle of dead leaves as he headed to the back fence, toward the gate to the alley. He could run, try to stay ahead of the cops, maybe double-back to Cheryl's car and make a break for it. But then what? He'd be on the lam, and before long, the entire force would be on the lookout for him.

He turned to the storage shed and ran his fingers over the lock, praying his father hadn't changed the combination. He spun the four dials, stopping at each number for the month and day of his mother's birthday, and pulled on the latch. It released. Nate slid the door open and then set the combo lock as best he could to appear it was still locked in place, and slid the door shut.

The sharp smell of gasoline struck him, the shelves along the back wall lined with the red jerrycans. One can sat on top of an old box of hard candy, one their mother had kept on her dressing table when they were young children, the sides and cover studded with images of the colorful sweets.

Nate moved the can off of it and opened the box's lid. A sweet cherry and mint aroma greeted him, still present after all these years, mixing with the odor of gasoline. Inside sat his gun, a SIG Sauer P320. He picked it up, his fingers wrapping around the grip. He pulled a magazine from the box and inserted it into the handgun, clicking it into place with his palm.

One shot and it could all be over. He'd done his research. Shooting in the head was for weenies because it doesn't always work. He could shoot himself into a vegetative state, his ass wiped by nursing staff for the rest of his life. Shooting in the chest is better, but angle it wrong and he could be seriously injured but alive, probably hooked to machines so he could breathe while his damaged lungs healed. If he healed enough to breathe on his own ever again. And then what? Jail?

No, it had to be a sure thing. The mouth. Far enough back that he is almost choking, so it doesn't blast through a cheek. Aim a little upward to get the brain. Blow it out. Never fails. With the gasoline, the gun might even ignite the whole shed, burn his body in an explosive blaze.

What a way to go. Just like Aunt Peggy wrote happened to him when he was eight before she traveled the time slip to save him. So, it would happen anyway, just eighteen years later. His father would probably love it, no longer having to deal with his loser son. Another room to empty into trash bags. Two rooms. His and Cheryl's. Let him set up a bar in one. A game room for the other. Maybe Peggy's could be a lounge. All his drinking buddies could come over, and they'd have a swell time.

He gripped the gun, its cool metal against his fingers and palm. He lifted it to his mouth, the muzzle a dark cyclops, the hollow eye waiting for its chance to blink with fire and metal.

The cherry-mint ghost from the candy box gave him pause. He imagined his mother, dressing for work, grabbing a candy from the box, her freshly painted fingernails, rose-pink, pulling at the stiff cellophane that crinkled as she unwrapped it, the smell as she popped one in her mouth, the aroma on her breath the rest of the morning. Cherry was her favorite, and she sometimes handed Nate his favorite, the yellow-brown butterscotch.

Nate lowered the gun. What would she think if she saw him now?

He put the gun back in the candy box and then pushed it under the shelves with his hands, behind him and out of sight. Outside, the distant crackle and chatter of the police dispatch sounded from the front of the house. They would be on him soon.

Nothing to do but wait. Or turn himself in, just like Dad told him to do.

Nate stood up, consoling his feelings of cowardice by reasoning that, if he lived, he could one day have another chance. He could, one day, rebuild the jabberwock and fix things right.

As he reached for the inner handle of the shed door, it slid open on its own with a rapid, grating rasp. Nate jumped back, raising his arms, expecting to see the figures of police officers, guns drawn, descending upon him. Instead, a single figure dashed inside, pushing Nate back and then sliding the door shut. A flicker of white light blinded Nate as the figure turned on a flashlight.

Nate blinked and looked away. When the light moved off his face, he looked up. His older self stepped toward him, his arms and neck snaked with tattoos while flame-like images licked up toward his scarred face. The older man held a gray rectangular object in one hand with the flashlight. "You really made a fucking mess of things, Natey boy," he said, and with his free hand, he slapped Nate across the face.

15

Nate stumbled back. The slap stung, but didn't hurt as much as the shock of being hit. He rubbed his cheek. "Fuck you."

"I've wanted to do that for five goddamn years." The older man leaned over and set the flashlight on the floor facing upward to illuminate the room before waving the flat rectangular object. "But no more time for warm greetings. You have work to do." He handed the object to Nate.

It looked like a closed laptop, except the top of it had a keyboard and there didn't appear to be any seam to open it up to a screen. Nate flipped it over, and the back side had no screen, either, so it wasn't a tablet.

The man fumbled with a pair of goggles that dangled from his neck. His thin fingers gripped around the strap as he lifted it over the gray bristles of his short-shorn hair, but his arms trembled, as if stiffness was making it a great effort. Nate noted a series of needle marks along the inner elbow of his right arm.

The man finally gave up and let his arms drop, pointing to the object in Nate's lap. "That, *pendejito*, is going to save my ass. *Our* ass."

Pendejito. Nate didn't know what that meant but was sure it was something bad. An insult. "So, what is this thing? A computer?"

"I haven't a lot of time to explain. Right now, Dan is talking to the cops, and we've got, maybe, ten minutes."

Outside, the police radio squawked, followed by garbled voices and static.

"He called the cops." Nate's throat choked as he stated the betrayal out loud.

"Yeah, all that 'fatherly' bullshit to keep me long enough for them to show up. I should have run instead of cornering myself in here, letting them catch me after just a ten-minute search of the property. Just another stupid, loser thing for me to do." He raised his arms and then winced. "Arthritis is a bitch, give me a hand with these." He pointed to the goggles.

Nate reached over and pulled the goggles over

the older man's head, untangling the strap from a second pair that still hung around his neck. "What happened? The trial, I mean."

"Long story short, ten years for involuntary manslaughter, which was better than the second-degree murder the prosecution tried to pin on me. Believe it or not, Dad testified on behalf of my character, my tragic loss as a child, the struggles to do better in life. Stuff as much about himself as it was about me. That, and the confused testimony of the star witness about what really went down helped my case. Was there just one Nate or two? Ha."

"Star witness?"

He reached over and knocked the back of Nate's head with his fingers. "Oh, come on, *pendejito*, who else? I gave you one simple instruction, you asshole. Remember that? Even got you the gun to do it with, paying good money for the under-the-counter service. Oh, they got me on that, too. 'Unlawful possession of a firearm used in the commission of a crime.' I tried to pin it on the guy at the pawn shop, but he claimed he never saw me or Pops. The asshole was right, of course. I never got the gun from him in this fucked-up reset. Maybe it vanished from his inventory, or a copy from this time stream was still there. I'll never know. Just another fucking law of time travel, it seems. Anything we take back will come back with us, if we have it in our possession. I should of dropped the damned thing when I fled. Stupid, stupid,stupid. There it was in my apartment, to be found and handed over to the police by the 'star witness.'"

Nate exhaled. "Rico."

The older man sneered. "Patrick fucking 'Rico' McVey. And all you had to do was kill the little fucker, like I instructed."

"I..." Nate shook his head.

"I know, *'poor suffering Rico'*." He pointed toward his forehead. "I have it all up here, now, you know. What I did when I was you, what happened before, what happened in all the different realities of my life. If I wasn't here, you'd feel different about poor little Rico in a few months. You'd be rotting in that special wing of Evercrest Heights, the one for murderers and rapists, dreaming of the day you can finally fix what you broke, believe me." He pointed to the goggles in Nate's hands. "Put those on."

Nate slipped them on, the strap holding them in place against his face. Earbuds dangled from the frame. The goggles seemed to be some sort of tech but were lightweight and far less bulky than VR goggles. "What are these for?"

His older self pushed a button on the side of the keyboard in Nate's lap and then put on his own pair of goggles. "Not much time to explain, but this is the latest and greatest in computer technology. Well, thirty-five years from this place in time."

The goggles illuminated and a computer screen formed in front of Nate's eyes, floating between him and the shed door.

"Wow."

The older man pointed to an icon that floated in the air between them. "When you tap that, you're off to the circus. I've made some special enhancements. Took me years to figure out the proper reverb, tremolo and timing of each chime and chord to enhance the specifics, but this will allow you to stay almost four hours without that 'focus on the present moment' bullshit. If you want to return sooner, I've programmed in a sequence of notes to trigger a return. Just use the song, *'be it ever so humble, there's no place like home'* and you'll find yourself back here. Just that one line."

"I have to *sing* that?"

"You can click your heels for all I care, but it's the *notes* that matter, not the words. I can't sing them myself or I'll be zapped out of here, along with my equipment, but you know the tune." The man reached behind Nate, grunting as he slipped his hand in the space under the shelves and pulled out the candy box with the handgun. "But enough with the fun stuff. You have a job to do, and we're almost out of time, if you pardon the pun." He pulled the gun from the box and held it by the barrel, the handle toward Nate.

"No." Nate scooted away from his older self.

"Don't be a dick, Natey boy. This is our one chance."

Nate didn't know which annoyed him more, Natey boy or *pendejito*. "What the fuck do you expect me to do?" Nate sat on his hands.

The older man took a deep breath, raising the gun as if to strike Nate, but then lowered it and glanced at his wristwatch. "We have probably five minutes, maybe less, so I'll be quick for the slow-witted. Now, listen up. You need to go back to the morning of the car accident. At Centennial Park North, right off the highway, standing across the road from the sundial fountain. You'll watch the accident happen and then run to the car. You'll have one job, just *one*, and that is to shoot Rico. He'll be in the back seat, but not for long. Shoot the kid in the head before he crawls over to the front seat."

Nate leaned against the shelves, trying to

distance himself from the older man in the narrow space. "You are fucking crazy, man." Computer screen icons floated between them and Nate wanted to throw off the goggles, but kept his hands under himself instead. "Do you know how little chance there is that this will work? It's gonna be chaos there, man. The smoke, the fire, the heat of it all. I can't…"

"I'll say it again, *pendejito*. You have just one fucking job, and that is to shoot and kill Rico. You can do that. Believe me." The older man pointed to his scarred face. "I've been there before, remember? Yeah, you have to act quickly, but once you shoot the little shit's head off, just hum our little tune and you'll be back, safe and sound."

"It's impossible."

"No, it isn't. You're just being a limp weenie. Think of what we'll gain. Mom will live. Dan will be a real father. Cheryl will be alive. I'll have Ellie back…"

"I can't do it, man. The fire… I don't want to come back like you." Nate nodded at the older man's scarred face.

"Just do it!" The older man swatted toward Nate, the computer icons dancing out of the way. "I got burned because of Rico. Take care of him and none of this happens. He was supposed to die that day!

Everything was good when he was dead and out of our lives!" The older man leaned back, slouching. "Then I had to go back and fix things for Mom, and here we are." He sat up straight and leaned toward Nate. "This is our one best chance to fix everything."

"You seem so sure of yourself. You go back and fix it."

He shook his head, exasperated. "*Pendejito*, you know I can't do that. No matter what I do with this software, I can't overcome the seventy percent law of time travel and go back far enough. Only you can do this. Only you." Nate didn't move, and his older self sighed and clicked his tongue. "Or, you can just sit there with your fingers up your ass and go to prison in five minutes."

Nate pulled his hands out from under himself and crossed his arms. "I can't shoot a kid."

The older man raised his hand and Nate flinched, expecting another slap. But he instead placed his hand on Nate's shoulder. "It's the only way, man. If it weren't for Rico, Cheryl would still be alive. She has kids! You're an uncle, man! And Dan will be a good father, one of the best. And even Peggy would still be alive, writing her books and making a name for herself. You'll get to marry to the best woman in the world, Ellie. And think of it. Mom would be alive. We'd have our whole life's history with her. All those great things we missed out on growing up. But because of Rico, our life went to shit. He came out of that accident alive instead of Mom. Instead of even his own mother. She tried to get him off Mom, and he kept both of them in the car until it was too late. They died because of him. He *killed* Mom, man. Then he killed Cheryl. Can't you get that?"

Nate considered his older self's words. Had Rico been responsible for his mother's death? Nate had been unconscious after the accident, so he couldn't see what happened, but did that little fuck keep her pinned in the car until it was too late? Rico came up with that first "M&M Day" when they were still kids, coercing Nate to steal Dad's whiskey to commemorate the deaths of their mothers. Was Rico covering for the guilt of his role in their deaths? Whatever it was, he encouraged Nate's first taste of booze, the initiation toward countless more. It was Rico's idea to drink to their mothers, year after year, not just on "M&M Day," but any time Nate could snitch a bottle of hooch from Dad's collection, starting him on the downward slide to be just like his father.

Yeah, when *had* Rico ever been good for him? When they were older, Rico always took Nate to the bars, encouraging him to drink, even after it was clear Nate had a problem. Then that asshole had the gall to fire him from his best job, starting Nate's spiral into unemployment and poverty. Sure, Rico said he felt bad, practically cried, and he played up how his prick of a father made him do it. Poor Rico.

He always had his injuries to play up, too. The useless hand, the shame of the scars he hid with long sleeves and collars. And he used that to encourage Nate to go drinking with him. Even when Nate tried to stop... and he *had* stopped, for *months*... he had a red coin, for chrissake... and that asshole came back and forced him off the wagon. On purpose. And then Rico hurt Cheryl.

If it hadn't been for Rico, Nate wouldn't have needed to go back in time to change anything, and Cheryl would still be alive. She would still be whole. But Rico... *Rico* made another mess of things. That asshole had only to go outside when Nate told him to, but he was too fucking stubborn... to fucking *arrogant*... to do what he was told. And then he ran away while Cheryl bled to death, wasting time before calling an ambulance from a fucking pay phone. Head injury or gunshot, each time it was the same. Cheryl was dead because of *him*. Because of *Rico*. Rico, who wasted no time finding Nate's gun and turning it in to the police. *Fucking Rico McVey*. Was Nate really going to let himself take the fall for everything?

Nate reached out and snatched the gun out of his older self's grip before stuffing it in the back of the waistband of his jeans. The cold metal stung against his back.

The older man smiled. "Good, you feel it. Don't you? The *hate*? Use it for the next hour, and everything will be peachy again."

Nate frowned. "You could have come earlier, when we had more time to plan this."

The older man shook his head as he picked up the device with the keyboard. "Nope, that was my mistake before, giving you too much time to think. This is best, when the heat's burning up your ass. No time for fucking ruminations. No time to overthink." He waved his hand over the keyboard and a new screen appeared. He pointed to an icon that floated between them, an animated clock in the belly of a tabby cat, resembling the poster in Cheryl's room.

Nate leaned in and read the name, *PeiPei_10.2.1.exe*. "Does this work like before?"

"Oh, better, much better. Like I told you, this will keep you where you go for up to four hours, and it'll get you there faster than a whore spreads her legs. Just concentrate on where you want to go, that morning of October seventeenth. Remember how Aunt Peggy wrote about being sent back to that moment after the car accident? She traveled in time *and* space. I knew it had to be something we were missing, an accident of circumstance as she sat with her therapist watching the light bar and listening to the singing bowls. It was a bitch to work out, but I finally got the right tonal specifications to let that happen. Just think of the park, of the sundial sculpture, and it being eight o'clock in the morning, just minutes before the crash. It will put you in that spot, on that morning and at that time."

Nate inhaled a deep breath. "Okay, then, let's rock and roll."

His older self pointed at Nate's feet. "Socks. Can't have you running into broken glass and metal without shoes."

Nate sighed. He slipped off his shoes, removed his socks, and put the shoes back on. "Let's do this, man," he grumbled, gritting his teeth. He kept his mind focused on Rico, on what he did, so his fury wouldn't fade.

A metallic rumble sounded from the house. The garage door opening. Clipped, monotone voices amid the crackle of radios.

The older man's face paled, and his voice dropped to a sharp whisper. "Shit, we've got about one minute, Natey boy. Remember, October seventeenth, eighteen years ago. *Concentrate!*" He reached over, put the buds into Nate's ears, and then reached toward the floating icon and tapped it with his index finger.

The icon spun to a blur, and Nate's view of the shed's interior vanished, replaced by a dark void that soon sparkled with the multicolored lights. The tones began chiming through the earbuds, and he felt a warm vibration tingle along his skin, sinking in deeper throughout his body. Nate concentrated on that long-ago morning, his mother hurrying him up. Lois had to drop the boys off at school on their way to work. They would be late if he didn't skedaddle.

Mixed aromas of cool mint and sharp cherry struck him. Mom's smell from the box of candy that lay next to him. This would bring her back, restore the life stolen from him. From all of them. He would get a whole life with her, growing up, her watching him graduate middle school, high school, and then college. Because he would take care of it, so Rico would never foul up their lives. He would take care of Rico. Her warm smile would greet Nate each morning as he grew up, and he thought of a memory he hadn't recalled in years, of him snuggled close to her on the sofa as she read to him from a book of nursery rhymes. A lovely, aching memory.

The hard metal of the gun in his waistband moved against his back as the chimes reverberated, the lights blinking and shimmering in multiple colors. Soon, he would take care of Rico, so he would never have fouled up their lives. Nate concentrated on his loathing of the man. Of the *child* who killed his mother and destroyed so many lives. His tingling body grew weightless, and he spun into the showers of light and sound.

16

Nate sits cross-legged on the floor as the lights vanish and the room emerges around him. The air's warmth strikes him and he feels the prickling of sweat beginning on his face. The light in the room shifts in waves of shadows, his nose twitching at the sharp, metallic smell of gasoline.

Like waking from sleep, Nate shakes his head to clear it. He's sitting on concrete, gray metal walls around him. The shed. He reaches to his face, pulling the goggles off and setting them on the concrete next to him. Had he fallen asleep? Where had his older self gone?

Something isn't right, and Nate remains still as a quiet panic settles over him—the cops. Yet it is silent outside the shed. And bright. Light shimmers from the cracks around the door and from the vents above shelves lined with Dan's gasoline. Very *clean* shelves. In fact, the floor is spotless, too, and the other shelves hold only a toolbox and some gardening equipment. They are no longer cluttered with hastily stuffed boxes of forgotten childhood toys or hardware scraps that might be useful one day.

Nate stands up, holding himself still for a moment while the blood flows down through his legs, until the lightheadedness passes. If his counterpart's improved jabberwock has worked, he should be in Centennial Park, not still in the storage shed. Something has gone wrong.

Nate pulls on the storage shed door, and it slides easily open, its handle not equipped with the lock that was once there. Nate looks up, his mouth dropping open as he gasps at the scene before him.

The backyard is like a small park, neatly trimmed grass and pruned hedges of boxwood and juniper, with lilac and hydrangea blooming along the edges of the tall redwood fence. Wind chimes jingle in a soft breeze from the shaded porch, lush green ivy adorning the wooden posts and framing a white wicker couch and chair arranged around a low wooden table. In the center of the lawn, the red metal frame of a swing set supports two swings that sway gently in the breeze, a slide attached to its side. Nate's childhood play set.

The sight strikes him with longing. He had almost forgotten the swings and slide, artifacts of a childhood that seem like another person's life. In a way, they are.

Nate starts as laugher peels from a short distance. A woman's voice is followed by more laughter. It is coming from the house, the open kitchen window. Nate can see movement inside, but only shadows, a glint of long hair, perhaps, as someone bends to open the oven.

He's a stranger here, whenever this is. An intruder. And he has a gun stuffed into the waistband at his back, hidden only by the gray T-shirt he wears. Nate pulls his eyes away from the yearning sites and stumbles to the back gate. He swings it open and escapes to the alleyway behind the homes.

The alley is paved with a layer of white gravel, the wood fences bordering the yards on either side and shimmering with fresh paint, the wood beams tall and sturdy. This is when the neighborhood is new with families moving in to raise their children at the idyllic suburban edge of the city. In twenty years or so, it will be swallowed by the city stretching its borders, this neighborhood crumbling in value as those who can afford it move to newer enclaves further out, away from the growing blight. Rico did the same with his father after high school, when McVey Land and Living became successful enough that they didn't have to live near the ghetto properties they rented to the down-and-out folks like Nate.

He adjusts the gun snuggled against his back as he reaches the end of the alley. He needs to figure out what to do. Or he could hum the tune now, go back, and start over. But the cops were almost upon them in the shed, and going back now would put him instantly in their grasp. There would be no opportunity to run the program again. He needs to figure out what to do now, whenever this "now" is.

He turns onto the long neck of the cul-de-sac. He will walk down and around, just some guy taking a walk through the neighborhood to get a perspective of what place in time he is. If this is the morning of the car accident, he needs to find another way to get to Centennial Park. Why didn't he just appear there, like the older man told him he would?

He slows his pace and almost stops dead in his tracks. His mom's car sits in the driveway, its red paint cherry bright in the sunlight. An odd sensation creeps from his belly to his chest and into his throat, a mixture of panic and longing. He crosses the street to avoid walking past the car, to get a sense of what is going on at the house without getting too close.

Then he sees the sign, set in the fresh pruned grass of the McVey's front lawn: Open House. Red, blue, and yellow balloons dance along the sign's edges, as if waving for him to walk closer. The carport is empty, and the windows gleam in the sunlight without any curtains or shutters. Nate walks up the red brick path along the driveway to the front door and peers through the living room window. Inside, the McVey house is vacant, the walls barren white surrounding the empty gray-silver carpet.

No one lives here. No one has ever lived here.

The realization falls over him like cold sand. He is too far back in time. The McVeys have yet to even move into the house. It is years before the accident. Years.

Hopelessness settles over Nate as his newest failure dawns on him. He went back too far and has four hours, perhaps, before he'll be forced back. Four hours before his return to an unchanged present and into the hands of the cops.

"Excuse me." A soft female voice behind him. "Sir?"

Nate turns around, and his knees buckle. A

young woman, her auburn hair blowing in the breeze, looks at him and blinks as if startled. In her arms she holds a young boy, three or four years old, who looks warily at Nate with icy eyes. The young woman lets out a startled laugh, a familiar laugh, one that trembles through Nate as he looks at her, unable to speak.

He is staring at his mother. The young boy squirming in her arms is him, perhaps three years old.

"Oh," he says.

The woman shakes her head quickly, as if to clear her mind. "I'm sorry, I didn't mean to startle you."

He had forgotten her Midwestern twang. The softness of her voice. Eighteen years since he last spent a moment in her presence, and all the memories seemed to flood him in a rush. She clicks her tongue, and a red lozenge shifts in her mouth. A sharp smell of sweet cherry reaches his nose. He shifts his legs to maintain his balance and tries to speak, but nothing makes its way to his throat.

"Are you here for the open house?" His mother's face reddens. Does she recognize Nate? The resemblance to his father? "Uh, Barbara? She's the realtor. She had to get some paperwork she forgot. She'll be back in a few minutes." She sounds embarrassed and looks away.

"Oh, okay." Nate inhales a deep breath. Tears sting at his eyes, and he prays none spill out as he struggles to keep his composure. *Oh, god, it's her. It's her. It's her. It's really her...*

She adjusts the boy in her left arm and grunts, extending her free hand. "I'm Kathy Johnson. I live across the street."

Nate shakes her hand, soft and warm. "Uh, Harry. Harry Styles." He winces.

She nods and looks at the boy. "This is Nathan. Can you say hi to Mr. Styles, honey?"

The boy leans into her shoulder and then puts a thumb in his mouth, but his eyes don't leave Nate. "I'm four years old," he says, his voice slobbery.

"Nathan's birthday was yesterday." She laughs.

Nathan. No one had called him by his birth name since… since his mother. The woman standing a foot away from him. A giddy lightness flutters in his chest, a lightheadedness swooning through his head as the sunlight glows like a crimson-gold halo through her hair. A porch support leans into Nate's arm and he catches it before he stumbles and falls.

Kathy doesn't notice, her attention shifting to a buzzing cell phone in her jeans pocket. She pulls the phone out and looks at the screen, sighing before taking the call. "Hi, Peggy." She mouths *excuse me* to Nate and then turns and continues her conversation.

"No, honey, I'm not mad at you… it's okay. You're busy. I should have reminded you it was coming up. Yes, he's with me now." She holds up the phone for little Nathan. "Aunt Peggy wants to wish you a happy birthday."

"Pei-pei!" Nathan smiles.

As she holds the phone to the boy's ear, she whispers to Nate, "My sister. She forgot to call him yesterday."

Nate nods, too mesmerized by the woman standing in front of him to say anything.

She pulls the phone from the boy. "Hey, Peggy, can I call you back in a few minutes? I'm outside. No worries, sweetie." She places the phone in her pocket and then puts the boy down and takes his hand. "It always gets so complicated with her," she says to Nate. "She thinks I'm mad at her. I think she's mad at me. We end up not talking for months…" She stops and chuckles, shaking her head. "I'm sorry. I don't know why I'm boring you with my family drama."

Nate smiles and shrugs, trying to find something to say but afraid he will start blubbering nonsense if he opens his mouth.

A nondescript white sedan pulls into the driveway and stops.

"That's Barbara," Kathy says, waving at the plump woman in a brown dress getting out with a cloth satchel slung over her shoulder. Kathy turns back to Nate. "It was nice meeting you. Maybe we'll be neighbors?" She smiles, and again Nate's memories emerge from his fogged past—that smile, so bright and warm, so long ago... The feelings threaten once again to send him toppling over. He gives her a brief wave and grabs the post for support. He watches as she turns and approaches Barbara, little Nathan walking beside her. The boy looks over at Nate, his thumb back in his mouth.

"Hi ya!" Barbara shouts to Nate from the driveway. She and Kathy talk to each other before Kathy looks back at him once more. Then she looks both ways and, holding Nathan's hand, crosses to her house.

Nate cannot move his eyes from his mother as she walks up the driveway, but Barbara reaches where he stands and extends a hand in greeting, apologizing for being late. Did he wait long? Nate shakes his head, forcing a smile as she unlocks the front door, babbling some small talk that an instant later he forgets. Before they step inside, he looks back to his childhood home, but his mother is gone.

Nate follows Barbara into the house, walking with her to the kitchen, where she places a portfolio of paperwork on the table. She talks about the kitchen and its modern features, keeping her hand in her the cloth bag still over her shoulder. Nate senses she is being cautions, and probably has something to defend herself with in the bag.

Nate doesn't pay attention to what she is saying but keeps himself facing toward her, fearing that if she sees him from behind, she will notice the outline of the gun. He nods and smiles as if he is absorbing what she tells him.

After a minute, another couple enter the house through the open front door, and Barbara looks relieved. Nate, grateful for the interruption of her spiel, mumbles he will check out the layout of the house. Barbara nods his way as she greets the young couple.

Nate heads for the rear front bedroom, the one that will become Rico's, the most familiar to him in the house. Empty, the room should look larger, but as Nate catches his breath, he is struck by how small it feels. He spent a lot of time in this room with Rico, playing video games or searching a bounty of internet porn on his computer (Nate figured out how to get him past the parental locks), just listening to music and watching television, and later drinking from a flask stolen from Mr. McVey's "man cave" den across the hall.

Nate glances out the window, hoping he can spot another glimpse of his mother. No such luck, but he continues looking toward the house he grew up in, two ponderosa pines towering over the front lawn. Nate had forgotten about those trees, which his father had to remove around the time Cheryl was born, due to some sort of root disease.

Cheryl. She isn't even born yet. Here, his family is one still at their beginning, still full of hope and anticipation for the future. Just over four years to go before all of that comes crashing to an end.

Nate taps his fingers against the windowsill. *Unless I act.* He's been in this time stream for about forty minutes, give or take a few. That leaves him about three hours to devise a plan.

First, he needs to get out of this house. Find out where Rico might most likely be on a day before his family moved in. Where had they lived before? Nate can't remember, if he had ever known. As far as he remembers, Rico always lived across the street, but how much does one remember from when they were four years old? They didn't really become friends until they were both in school, and even then Rico was a year ahead of him. Until the accident. Months in the hospital kept him back a year, so he and Rico were in the same class after that. They became friends, really, only after that.

Their mothers were friends, first as neighbors and then as coworkers at a downtown credit union. That led to their morning routine, getting Nate and Rico to school before heading to their jobs. Except that one morning, Aunt Peggy was with them. Visiting for the week, she planned on shopping downtown.

Rico was a pest, complaining that Nate, sitting in the middle of the back seat, was taking up too much room. Peggy tried scooting over on her side to give Nate some more room, but he was determined to stand his ground with Rico, spreading his legs and arms out to annoy the kid.

The same kid he needs to find. Now. He can find a library, perhaps, with computers he can use. Find out where they are living and pray it is close enough to find in time before Nate is whisked back to his present, the cops at the door of the shed, ready to arrest him.

It seems impossible odds. Looking out at the green lawn and tall trees of his childhood home, the white exterior paint bright and fresh, the glowing paint of his mother's car sparkling in the sunlight, Nate knows he has to at least try.

Just as he is about to turn from the view, a large

sedan the color of blue twilight pulls up in front of the house. Nate catches his breath, his heart pounding in his chest. He recognizes this car. It is *the* car. From the accident.

When the front doors open and a man and woman emerge, Nate exhales, and his plan comes into focus.

Geoffrey McVey, wearing a business suit, stretches as he looks toward the house. Behind him, Lois McVey opens the back door, and a young boy hops out, about five years old, dressed in a red checkered shirt and cowboy hat.

Rico.

Nate can't believe his luck, the coincidence of it all. What are the chances... Then it strikes him. Those last moments in the shed with his older self, he smelled the candy, reminding him of his mother reading to him, all while thinking of the accident that killed her, and the boy, Rico, who made it happen. Somehow, the improved jabberwock program got him to a period of time when all those things came together. This is that moment. He can still fulfill his plan and fix the timeline, per his older self's instruction.

Kill the kid. Kill Rico McVey.

17

Nate recognizes the booming deep voice of Geoffrey McVey as he enters the house, introducing himself. "My wife came here yesterday, wants me to see the place."

Nate stands at the bedroom door, looking out toward the family room and kitchen where Barbara is touring the younger couple. She turns to Geoffrey, who is out of Nate's line of sight.

"Oh, yes, I remember! Come join us, I was just showing the kitchen…"

"I'm on my lunch break. Can you give me the short version?"

Barbara looks flustered. "Oh, well…"

"I told him everything you were kind enough to show me yesterday," Lois says, with a false cheer in her voice. "A quick walk-through would be ideal."

"Oh, absolutely." Barbara turns to the young couple. "You can follow, if you like, and I can answer your questions later."

As she talks, Geoffrey and Lois step into view, along with little Rico. Nate backs into the bedroom, his mind racing. *What do I do? What should I do?* He could step out now, fire the gun at Rico, and as pandemonium ensues, hum the stupid ditty to get him back home. Assuming it would work. Should he trust his older self that it would work? But why would he tell him something that wasn't true? This is as much for him as it is for Nate.

The group reaches the hallway, the realtor's voice loud as she explains the home's four bedrooms down the hall. They reach the room, and Nate backs into the bedroom closet, pretending to examine its interior. He forces a smile and waves as the group enters the doorway. The younger couple hovers behind Barbara as Geoffrey pushes his way to the front.

Nate had forgotten the man's height and muscular girth. Geoffrey moves through the room as he examines the carpet, the window, barely acknowledging Nate as he approaches the closet where he stands, hovering a good six inches over Nate's height.

"Seems small." He glances at Nate, a flicker of a smile on his lips. "The house, for what's being asked."

"Oh, but this is the smallest room in the house," Barbara says. "As you can see, it is perfect for a child's room or nursery, with a beautiful view of the street."

"Well," Lois says in a quiet voice, "it could also be a home office, Geoffrey."

Geoffrey scoffs and turns to his wife. "You planning to keep an eye on me twenty-four-seven?"

Her face turns red, but she laughs and flicks her hand toward Geoffrey, as if brushing off the comment as a joke.

He rolls his eyes and turns toward Nate, pushing in close so Nate has to back into the closet to keep his personal space. His eyes look him up and down. Nate can sense the man taking him in. Jeans, T-shirt, ratty shoes.

"You don't seem like someone interested in a place like this," he says to Nate. "You working for an investor? Planning to buy this out from under us?"

Nate shakes his head, keeping his back to the wall. The gun scrapes along the plaster. "I'm waiting for Ellie," he says, hoping to deflect attention from the sound. "My wife." *Ellie*. Odd how that name came foremost in his mind without even thinking.

Geoffrey grunts and grips Nate's shoulder with a

thick hand. "I'm just joshing you." He shakes Nate's shoulder but then lets go and turns to Barbara. "Show me the rest. Impress me."

"Absolutely," Barbara says, and as they continue into the hall, she mentions the growing neighborhood and all the young families and excellent schools that entails. The group heads back toward the family room.

Nate's hands tremble. He reaches back and adjusts the gun more securely in his waistband. It almost slipped out when he hit the wall. Nothing like a fully loaded SIG Sauer handgun falling through his pants leg for all to see.

Rico emerges from the hallway, pointing a toy pistol. The boy looks startled for a moment, as if he expected the room to be empty after the adults left. He points the gun at Nate. "Bang, bang."

"Hey, there," Nate says. He tries to think fast. The kid is right there, right in front of him, but he can't bring himself to reach for his gun. Instead, he smiles and waves at the kid.

"You're supposed to be dead," Rico says, pointing the plastic pistol again. "Bang, bang!"

Nate's hands grow cold. "Hey, that's a nice gun you have." He takes a step forward. "You like guns?"

The boy frowns at Nate. "Aww, you're supposed to be dead."

Nate presses a hand against his shoulder and falls to his knees. "Ouch! Yeah, you got me, Rico, but it's just a flesh wound."

The kid looks at Nate warily. "I'm Patrick."

Nate nods. "Sorry, you look like a Rico to me."

The boy shakes his head but smiles. "Patrick."

"Okay," Nate says, leaning forward, his heart thumping. The voices of the others are still down the hall, moving from the family room to the kitchen. He has only a minute, perhaps. Now or never.

Nate swallows. "Well, Patrick, do you want to see a real gun?" He reaches to his back, pulling the handgun from his waistband and, holding it by the handle, points it toward the child.

The boy's eyes widen as he smiles. He reaches a hand up but then pulls it back.

"It's okay," Nate tells him. "You can touch it."

"Father says not to."

Nate feels his face growing as cold as his hands. "It's okay," he says, moving his finger to the trigger. "I won't tell."

The boy reaches up a tentative hand, placing a fingertip on the top of the gun before pulling it back. He looks at Nate and smiles.

Nate's hand trembles, the weapon's barrel quivering inches from the boy's face. He tries to generate the hate he had felt just a short time ago.

Everyone he cares about will die or be irrevocably hurt by this little monster. This is his chance to stop that from happening. Just a little more pressure...

"Patrick!" Geoffrey's voice, coming up the hall.

The boy starts and steps away from Nate.

Nate, shivering, pulls his hand back and then stuffs the gun back into his jeans waistband. He backs toward the closet, an index finger on his lips, showing the boy not to say anything. Nate steps into the closet and slides the door halfway shut.

So close... so close. Nate's heart pounds in his ears, and the sharp coolness of a tear cuts down his face.

As Geoffrey McVey enters the room, Nate can't tell if he is feeling anger or relief. He trembles as he struggles to control his breathing and remain quiet. *So goddamned close.*

Nate can see them through slats in the closet door. Rico stands up straight, his head craning upward to look at his father. The kid is dwarfed by the man's height.

"What have I told you about wandering off?"

"I'm not supposed to." Rico's voice is meek, but he keeps standing straight.

Lois calls from the kitchen. "Geoffrey, be easy on him."

"I'm handling it," Geoffrey says. Then he closes the bedroom door and looks down at Rico. "Wipe that smile off your face."

Nate can see the boy's face in profile, and his expression isn't a smile but a grimace of fear—an expression familiar to Nate from years of witnessing Rico confronted by his father.

Geoffrey kneels down in front of Rico. "Or do I have to wipe it off myself?" He slaps the boy across the face with the flat of his palm.

The child's cheeks burn red and his lips tremble. His fingers twitch at his side. He sniffles.

Geoffrey points a finger at Rico's face, his other hand raised and angled, like a hawk eager to claim its prey. "Don't cry."

Rico sniffs, his lips thin and frowning.

He slaps the boy again. *"Don't cry."*

Rico's chin trembles.

"Girls cry. Are you a girl, Patrick? Should I call you Patty from now on?" He slaps the boy's face again. "Don't cry."

A tear snakes down the boy's face.

Slap! "Don't cry, Patty."

The child stands up straighter. His fingers no

longer twitch and he is stiff as a soldier, but his frowning mouth continues to tremble.

Geoffrey continues his taunt. "Is that what I should call you now? *Patty?*"

The boy's left leg shakes as another tear slips down his face.

"Don't." *Slap!* "Cry." *Slap!*

Geoffrey's chest moves in short, quick breaths, his face red.

The boy's face grows stone cold, his skin pale. He stops shaking and stares back at his father without expression.

Geoffrey nods. "You remember that, *Patty.* You do as I say and don't wander off. Right?"

The boy doesn't respond, his eyes looking past his father at the white wall behind him.

"Geoffrey!" The door swings open and Lois steps inside. Rico remains motionless, not responding to his mother's entrance.

Geoffrey stands up, brushing his hands against his thighs as if he had just been digging in the dirt. "What?"

Lois grabs Geoffrey's arm and pulls him into the hall. "I overheard those kids. They're going to make an offer. I want this house, Geoffrey."

"The one on Chestnut has a larger yard for a pool."

"It also only has three bedrooms and a smaller kitchen." Lois turns to the boy. "You okay, Patrick?"

The boy slowly turns to his mother and nods. "Yes'm." His voice is distant but firm.

"Stay here," she tells him and then pulls Geoffrey down the hall. She continues talking, her voice fading as she takes her husband outside the family room's sliding door to the backyard where the realtor is talking to the young couple.

The boy remains standing in his spot, his blank eyes returning to the white wall.

Nate is shaking in the closet. Memories deep in the darker regions of his mind reveal themselves. *The piano Rico loved, a gift from his mother, being carted off, Rico standing pale and expressionless. "It's a girl thing," Geoffrey says, "be glad for your gimpy hand that you can't play anymore." Geoffrey returning from work early one summer afternoon while Rico and Nate stand in their carport, wearing swimsuits, Nate helping him fix his bicycle. Geoffrey telling his son, "Cover that ugly alligator skin and clean up this mess." Moments later, Nate watching from across the street as Rico moves his bicycle to the rear of the carport, facing away from Geoffrey, who pulls off his belt and cracks it across his son's scarred back. Rico stands up straight but doesn't cry out, a red welt forming at an angle down his back...*

Many memories over the years of the tornado of fury that is Geoffrey McVey. Nate just accepted it, as Rico never made a deal out of it, not outwardly. No wonder he became the man he did.

Geoffrey McVey is the monster, not Rico. Not this little boy.

Nate pulls the gun out and considers following Geoffrey and shooting him in the back of the head. Yes, that is what he should do. That is what that thug deserves. A cowardly thug, picking on a boy. Even as a teen and young man, Rico was never a match for his father. Not with his injuries or his broken soul.

The boy continues to stand rock still, staring at the wall. No, Nate can't do this to him. Shoot his father, ugly bully that he is, right in front of him. The boy has had enough trauma already.

Nate places the gun on a shelf in the closet, not trusting himself to refrain from its use if he comes across Geoffrey McVey again in the next few minutes.

He leaves the closet and kneels beside Rico. "Hey." He tries to keep his voice soft and to control the tremble he feels inside.

The boy doesn't respond. His face is pale and smooth, showing no sign of being slapped. Nate cringes. *Geoffrey knew just how to do it without leaving marks.*

"Hey, Rico." He puts his hand on the boy's shoulder.

Rico flinches and blinks. Nate pulls away, raises his hands palms up as a gesture of surrender, but then remembers what his father just did and puts his hands down at his sides. Low and nonthreatening.

The boy looks at him, askance. "Patrick."

Nate smiles. "Right, I'm sorry, buddy. You could be a Rico, though. Pat-*Rick*. Rico. Get it?"

The boy's face remains without expression, but Nate thinks he sees a flash of a smile on the corners of the boy's lips. "He had no right to do that to you, Rico. He was wrong."

Rico wipes at his nose with his knuckles. "I was bad."

"No, you weren't. Even if you were, what he did was wrong." Nate feels his throat choking up. "I stood by while he did that, and that was wrong, too. I'm sorry, Rico. All those times. This time, especially."

Rico looks at Nate with narrowed eyes. His fingers clench and unclench at his sides.

"I know. I'm not making sense," Nate says, trying to maintain a smile, but his mouth feels tight and his chin trembles. "You know, buddy, even grown-ups cry. Even grown-up men." A tear flickers down Nate's face and he swipes it away. "Sometimes, it's good to cry. That's better than holding it all inside so we become as bad as they are."

The boy jerks as he takes a sharp breath, his eyes pooling.

Nate nods at him. "It's okay, buddy. Never let a bully like that make you think you are anything less than you are."

The boy's body heaves in silent gasps, and he falls toward Nate, who catches him in a bear hug. Young Rico cries in Nate's arms.

"Yeah, that's good, young man. Really good. Let it go." Nate cries too, so the child isn't alone in his tears. He cries for the two of them, for everything he saw Geoffrey do to him, everything he didn't see, and all the grief he knows is yet to come to this little boy's life.

18

They find Geoffrey and Lois on the back porch of the house with Barbara. The young couple huddles in a far corner of the yard.

Nate holds Rico's hand as they approach his mother.

She turns and looks exasperated. "Oh, Patrick." She looks up at Nate. "What has he done now?"

"Nothing," Nate says, struggling to add a lilt of cheer to his voice. "I found him alone in one of the rooms and thought you might have lost track of him."

Lois takes Rico's hand from Nate's. "Oh, honey, I told you to wait." Looking back at Nate, she adds, "I told him to stay inside, but thank you anyway."

Nate shrugs. "Okay. He seemed a little lost is all."

"Honey, your eyes are all puffy." Lois pulls a facial

tissue from her purse and wipes his eyes. "Have you been crying?"

Geoffrey's shadow moves over Lois and Rico. "It's allergies, Lois." His eyes flare at his son, but Rico takes no notice of him and hugs in closer to his mother.

Nate glares at Geoffrey. "Yeah, those *allergies* are savage." He's glad he didn't bring the gun out with him or he might have lost control.

Geoffrey pulls a cigarette from his jacket pocket and lights a match with a sharp strike. He loses his grip on the matchbook, and it falls into hydrangeas bordering the back patio. "Aw, shit." He kicks at the bush and then turns back to Nate. "Well, your business with us is done, I assume?" He flashes Nate his best "fuck you" smile, one Nate has seen many times. Or will. "I would like to continue my conversation with this nice lady and my wife. Thank you for bringing out my son."

Nate nods and then winks at Rico before going back inside the house. He watches through the sliding glass door as Rico clings to his mother's side, one arm lifting with his thumb extended, as if he wants to suck it but doesn't. The boy glances over to the glass, sees Nate, and smiles.

Lois McVey is very motivated to get this house, and Geoffrey makes his proposal. Minutes later, Barbara explains to Nate and the young couple that he offered over the asking price, and that she is closing the open house early.

The young couple looks disappointed. Nate feels numb. Barbara escorts all of them to the front porch, thanking them for stopping by.

Nate watches as Lois opens the back door of the car so Rico can slide into his seat. The boy glances over at Nate and gives him a brief wave. Nate waves back. A deep melancholy dumps over him as the car drives up the street and out of sight.

Nate helps Barbara pull out the open house sign and load it into the trunk of her car before bidding her farewell. When she realizes he is on foot, she offers to drive him wherever he is headed, if it is in her direction.

"Nah," Nate says, "The fresh air will do me good." He wants to get away and be alone in his failure.

He turns and heads up the street, a wave of sadness continuing to roll through him. *I changed nothing. Everything will happen as it had before.*

He failed. Again. It is a small consolation that Nate feels little regret. It wasn't right to kill the child. If only there were another way, but he can't see it. Because he spared the child, when he hums the stupid tune, or just waits out to the deadline of his place in this time stream, he will be in the hands of the cops. Even his older self won't be able to stop it. Maybe it is what has to be. Maybe his punishment will be justice for what happened to Cheryl, for he has failed his sister most of all. He deserves what is to come.

He turns, looking back at the house he grew up in. His mother's car is gone from the driveway, probably off to the grocery store, little Nathan sitting in the cart basket facing her. A young family, still growing, full of promise and hope. The brief glory will last, perhaps, the next five years, before that unending nightmare will take its place.

Nate turns and continues up the street. If only the McVeys had never moved in. His mother would never have carpooled with Lois. The accident would never have happened. He never would have known Rico. Cheryl would never have known him. Everything would have been better.

Nate stops at the corner and looks back. A notion creeps into his mind, a small spark that blooms in an instant to the full conflagration of an idea that is as simple as it is ingenious.

Of course!

Nate hurries to the top of the street and turns

down the alley that runs behind the houses. *Why didn't I think of this before?*

This will work. He is certain of it. The solution has been there the whole time. And no one, especially an innocent child, will have to die.

Moments later, Nate enters the yard through the back gate. No one is home, so Nate isn't concerned about anyone seeing him. The shed, his entry point to this fresh and forgotten past, sits in the shade of a sycamore. Its door has no padlock. His father didn't put one on until a summer when someone started stealing his gas cannisters.

He slides open the door and steps inside. *Two should do it.* He grabs a five-gallon jerrycan and pulls it down. The weight is more than he expected, and he struggles to maintain his grip as it thumps down to the concrete floor. *Well, maybe one will do.*

He lugs it up, the liquid gas sloshing inside. He would prefer to just take it with him across the street, but he can't risk anyone seeing him and stopping him. He will take the longer way around through the alley. He doesn't bother shutting the shed door. Dad will just get his padlock earlier than before.

He holds the handle with his right hand, reaching down with his left to secure the base, and dashes through the alleyway, the white gravel crunching beneath his shoes. He feels a blister forming on his heel, the sacrifice of not wearing any socks, but the earlier cuts from his recent forays into the past don't bother him much at all. He is on a mission that will soon be completed.

The cannister feels heavier as he rounds the horseshoe-shaped alley bordering the cul-de-sac, but he is almost at his destination. Hidden by back yard fences, he can enjoy the birdsong from the trees lining the yards beyond. He feels safe and upbeat, the coming end to his misery and restoration of a life he never even dared to imagine feeling, for the first time, a reality.

He reaches the house, soon to be the McVeys, in a short time. He reaches over the gate to the latch, but it won't budge. Feeling with his fingers, he touches the square bulb of a padlock. He won't be able to enter through the gate. Shit.

He sets down the can and thinks. The fence is about six feet tall, but he could scramble over it and hope no neighbors notice. But how would he get the jerrycan into the yard? He won't be able to open the gate from the inside, either.

Nate ponders for a minute, his cheerful mood

fading. *So close.* He can think of only one solution. He will need to drop the can over the fence and hope it doesn't burst open. Standing on a horizontal slat, he peeks over the gate. The yard is grass, thank god, so should give the cannister a soft landing.

He picks up the can and heaves it over the edge of the gate, one hand on the handle and holding the cannister horizontally as he scoots it along the top edge until it balances over to the other side. Nate miscalculates the point of gravity and it pulls down the other side, dropping sooner than he expected. His grip on the handle slips, his fingers releasing the cannister. The shift of weight causes him to lose his foothold on the horizontal beam and fall backward.

He hits the ground on his side, the pain unnoticed under a spasm of panic that rips through him. *What if it explodes?* The jerrycan thumps hard on the other side. He hears a sloshing sound at the point it landed, but no explosion and no sharp scent of spilling gasoline. It survived the plunge.

His mood buoyed, he jumps up and peeks over the gate. The cannister sits in the grass, red against the deep green carpet, undamaged. He pulls himself up over the gate and, scraping his arms, and scrambles over the rough top edge and into the yard, careful to keep his feet from stepping on the cannister.

He lies on his back for a moment, the grass itching at his back. He doesn't care. *Almost done.*

He stands up, grabbing the cannister, and relieved no unseen leaks reveal themselves, he carries it to the patio and sets it down near the hydrangeas. He puts his hands into the bushes, parting them and searching until his eyes catch his prize, a bit of thin cardboard. He plucks it out of the bushes and grips it between his fingers. The matchbook Geoffrey had dropped earlier, an image of a bird, its wings spread and head turned in profile, with Thunderbird Lodge written underneath. Three matches remain on the comb.

Nate puts the matchbook in his jeans pocket and carries the gas cannister to a bedroom window that would become Geoffrey's den and home bar. Rico had discovered the locked room had an easy entrance from the backyard. The window had never been properly installed, and a little jiggling on the lower sash would release the window latch. Nate presses his palms against the glass and moves them quickly until he hears a faint clink, and the window starts moving upward. Bingo!

Nate enters the room through the window, grabbing the gas cannister and pulling it in after him. He unscrews the cap and begins pouring gasoline over the carpet, splashing some more over the walls. He proceeds through the rest of the house, leaving a steady stream of gasoline from room to room, careful not to spill too much out in any one spot until he has spread it throughout the structure. He splashes the remaining gasoline onto the walls as high as he can get and then more onto the carpets of the living and family rooms.

He drops the cannister in the middle of the hallway. No need to take it out with him. The smell is harsh, and he feels the sharpness in his lungs. Time to go.

Nate leaves the house the same way he came in. He sniffs his hands and clothes to ensure he didn't spill any fuel on them and, satisfied he will not explode, he strikes a match.

It flares to life. He flicks it through the open window and steps back. Nothing. He steps forward and looks through the window. The burned out match lies on the carpet.

"Dammit!" he hisses, careful not to be too loud and attract attention from over the fence.

He pulls himself back inside through the window. Two matches to go. He winces at the sharp smell of gasoline. He'll need to light a match close to the middle of the room, where the steel-gray carpet is sopped. He kneels down and then strikes the match. The match tip scrapes off and falls to the floor.

One left.

"No, no, no..." He can't fail now. He is so close. Nate rips the last match from the comb, takes a deep breath, and strikes. It flares to life. Careful not to blow the flame out with his breath, he ignites a corner of the cardboard packaging to kindle the fire. Protecting the flame with one hand, Nate reaches out to place the burning matchbook on the gas-soaked carpet.

The fumes over the carpet explode in a flash. Nate jumps back, his hands stinging, and falls against the back wall. The fire snakes along the line of fuel, some creeping up the walls and bursting where he had splashed the gasoline. The heat scrapes against his face and prickles through his clothes.

Gasping, he rushes to the window and pulls himself through, grunting at the pain growing in his hands. He falls to the brick patio and brushes at his jeans and shirt in case there are any flames. They are hot, but not burning. He is safe.

Nate walks to the center of the backyard, and then turns to the house. Smoke pours out of the bedroom window, and he can see from the family room sliding door that the flames have traveled down the hallway and are quickly engulfing the rooms.

"Yes!" he shouts. He no longer cares if anyone hears him. He clenches his hand and fist-pumps. "Fucking yes!"

A sharp pain slices through his fist and he opens his fingers. His hand is reddened and blisters are forming where the fire caught him before he fled the house. Not too serious, he hopes, but will need some treatment when he gets to his new life. Excitement grows in his chest at the thought. A new life.

He did it. It is done. The McVeys will never move into this house. They can get the one on Chestnut, wherever that was. Hopefully far away from Autumn Lane. Far away from the Johnsons. His family is, at last, safe.

Nate is ecstatic as the flames surge and spurt from every window. He steps further back as the heat grows and heavy, black smoke swirls up into the sky. In the distance, Nate can hear the sounds of sirens. It is time to go home.

Home. Into the life he should have had all along. Things will be as they always should have been. It is, at last, accomplished.

He raises his arms and sings with the enthusiasm of an operatic baritone, a loud and booming voice harmonizing to the roar of flames. "Be it ev-er so hum-ble..." He taps together the heels of his tennis shoes for good measure. "There's no-o place like home!"

The sky flashes, churning from day to night and back to day again. The air shifts from cold to warm and back again as the dizzying sensation of an invisible vortex rushes around him. He feels it. The time streams are merging. His changes are taking root, changing the years—decades!—from this event forward, altering lives of everyone whose life he has just affected. Nate whoops with joy, but his cry is cut short. Darkness invades, black as the thick smoke of the burning house. The ground vanishes from beneath him and Nate is pitched into a black abyss, falling deeper and deeper, and his earlier glee shifts to terror as he is certain he will never reach the end.

Nate screams.

19

He woke to the clanging of bells. His head splitting with pain, Nate wrapped himself tighter in the worn denim jacket, still damp from an earlier rainfall. He could see the pitched tip of the clock tower from his vantage behind the restaurant and counted eleven chimes. His stomach growled, anticipating the possibility of food while the kitchen wrapped up for the night.

He shivered, the sensation of falling from a great height still tormenting him. His dreams were darkest when he had the shakes. He looked down at the shattered Jack Daniels he had knocked back that evening, trying to remember how he got to the alley behind the restaurant where he passed out.

An alley. It seemed a part of his dead sleep delirium. He was carrying something heavy. Then a fire. A large, warm fire. He felt happy in that dream. He tried to invoke it, perhaps lose himself back to it, but the door to the kitchen swung open and out stepped a man in an apron, carrying a gray trash cannister to the dumpster.

Nate attempted a smile, the bristles of his thick beard prickling against his face. He put his hands out with slow deliberation. "Any food you can spare?"

The man halted, looking Nate up and down as he crinkled his nose. "No, get out."

Nate recognized the man as the owner, Luigi. The man used to give him lollipops as a child when Nate's family dined here, one of his mother's favorite spots. Hunger twisted his stomach. "Scraps?" He eyed the cannister the man held.

Luigi rolled his eyes and finished his trek to the dumpster, tossing the contents inside. "Help yourself." He turned and stepped closer to Nate. "I give you five minutes. Then I call the cops."

"Thank you. God bless you." Nate had long ago learned to make do with humiliations disguised as small favors, but he didn't feel thankful and certainly didn't believe in god. He headed to the dumpster to dig through the refuse.

Luigi watched and then spat on the ground. "*Spazzatura!*" He disappeared into the bright kitchen and shut the door.

Nate's hands hurt as he fished through the refuse, looking for remnants of pasta and meat near the top before it could slither down to the spoiled foods sitting since that afternoon. Competing with the flies, he ate. He licked his fingers and palms to get every bit he could manage, wincing over the stinging in his hands that felt like a knife slicing into his flesh.

The pain overcame his hunger after a couple of minutes, and he walked to the light over the kitchen door to look at his hands. Red and blistered, they looked burned. They had been fine that morning. What had he done to himself during his afternoon blackout?

He put his hands under his arms and walked down the alley, trying to ignore the pain. The few bucks he hustled the day before were spent, but maybe he could score something tonight if his usual plug would cut him a break. He might spot Nate a dime, if he was in a charitable mood. Enough to calm the ache in Nate's bones and the sickness coiling in his gut. But in the dead hours of a weeknight, the scant pittance Nate might have to settle for was a bottle of hooch. That, at least, might take his mind off his stinging, trembling hands.

Nate kept walking to stay ahead of the patrolling cops, turning toward the abandoned tracks that cut through downtown and would lead him to his usual campsite behind TJ's Minute Mart. Sometimes the mini-mart's late-night regulars would spare him a can of Coors or a bag of chips.

He followed the warped wooden ties holding rusted steel rails drowning in weeds. Nate trembled from the growing need for that elusive fix, a buzz that led to precious darkness and, perhaps, a favored dream. A breeze kicked up, and he shuddered in his still-damp clothes. He wrapped his hands under his arms, the blisters stinging against the rough cloth. The vision of a warm bonfire burning in front of him seemed like a fine place to return to.

He passed the backside of a group of single-floor apartments, soft yellow light glowing from behind the barred windows. Colorful lights twinkled in a breezeway between two buildings.

Tarsha is working tonight.

Nate had no idea where the thought came from, but with it came a clutter of disconnected thoughts, unrelated images around this apartment building. He turned toward the lights, his feet leading him away from the tracks. A feeling crept over him, a deep melancholy of nostalgia, and he felt drawn like a gnat to the lights twinkling in the shadows.

They lined a curtained window, flickering diodes that produced in Nate the strange image of a laptop computer with glowing wires protruding from the sides. Nate shook his head to dispel the image, for with it came a taut thrum, winding like a steel wire in his gut. He turned to leave and go back to the tracks, to TJ's and his spot behind the dumpsters.

Nate froze. A chill crawled up his spine at the sight of a car parked in front of the apartment diagonal to the one with the lights. An old, dark-colored Lexus, clean and well-kept, stood out among the junkers parked around it. The paint gleamed in light escaping between the brown curtains over the apartment's front window. The car glowed with a familiarity that sparked the first moment of excited curiosity Nate had felt in a long time. He stepped toward the car, close enough he could read the license plate in the dim light. The white letters of the vanity license plate confirmed his suspicion: MCVLALI. *McVey Land and Living.*

He knew this car. He used to work with the owner in his distant past life, just over two years earlier before his destitute life on the streets. He must have wandered into one of the company's properties.

The car sat in front of apartment 8, and a sense of unease hummed in Nate's gut as he looked at the door, as if a terrible memory lurked behind it. His knees weakened and he leaned against the rear of the car for support.

Nate jolted backward as the screeching whistle of the car's alarm cut through him. Instinctively, he spun and bolted, running headlong into the breezeway's metal support pole. His knees gave out as pain cracked through him, and he sank to the concrete walkway. The door to apartment 8 swung open, and a man emerged, his thick, curly hair catching the light from inside as his eyes darted about, finding Nate crumpled at the base of the pole.

Nate looked up at the man, his mind flowing with disconnected thoughts, unrelated images that skulked out of his mind with teeth and claws. His mother's bell jar clock. An older man yelling at him. A young woman in a hospital room. These thoughts revolved around this one face, one he hadn't seen in almost two years. Yet here he was, as if showing up on cue, drawn to this moment like the turn of a clock's hand.

"Rico," Nate said, his eyes wide. "It's me, Nate."

The man took a step back and then clicked a fob that turned off the shrieking alarms. "Get out of here," he said.

"It's me. Nate. Do you remember?"

The man shook his head. "I'm five seconds from

calling the cops. Now get going." He waved his left hand, which gripped a compact Smith & Wesson pistol.

"No, Rico!" Nate looked into the man's eyes and raised his hands in surrender. "Please, it's me, Nate Johnson!"

The man's eyes squinted as he looked down at Nate. "I don't…" He paused, tilting his head to the side. "Accounting?"

Nate nodded and smiled, relaxing his hands a bit. "Yes! It's been a while. I know."

The man stuffed the gun in his back pocket and stepped toward Nate. "Yeah, this is a weird surprise. I didn't recognize you with the beard. What's it been? Two years?"

Nate nodded. "Sorry for fucking things up."

The man looked at the car. "It's fine, no harm done."

Nate shook his head. "I meant back in accounting. But, yeah, sorry for that, too."

The man smiled. "I think it scared you more than it did me." He reached out his hand toward Nate. "So, how goes it, Mr. Nate Johnson?"

Nate took his hand and let the man pull him up. He winced from the pain of the grip over his blisters. "Been better."

The man sniffed and then exhaled sharply. "So it seems."

Nate's teeth chattered. "Sorry."

"Hey, no problem, no problem. But let me see your hand again."

Nate held both jittering hands out. "I don't know what I did."

"Shit, dude. You need to get those treated. Come inside."

Nate followed the man to the doorway. "Thanks, Rico."

The man paused, turning to Nate. "Why do you call me Rico?"

Nate felt his face blush and shook his head. Why *did* he call him Rico? He knew the man's name was Patrick. Patrick McVey. The nickname seemed to reach out from the fog in his mind, clawing at his brain the same way as he saw the colored lights and then the car. He chuckled, for if he didn't, he feared he would cry. "I don't know, man. Sorry."

Patrick nodded. "No problem." He hesitated, as if to say more, and then walked inside the apartment. "Let's take care of those hands."

A somber dread rolled over Nate as he looked through the doorway. "Saint Teresa's isn't too far, maybe you could drive me there?"

"No way, man. You'll be waiting in the ER for hours. Come inside."

Nate followed Patrick inside. The comfortably warm room smelled of bleach and soap, plus an aroma like new carpeting. The studio had a kitchen to the left of the door, a bathroom in the back, and a main area dominated by a double-bed in the center. Other than that, it had little furniture, just a small table next to the bed and two stools at the kitchen counter. Nate's sense of gloom eased, an odd familiarity with the room's layout calming his anxiety.

"Welcome to my private escape," Patrick explained. "Not a great part of town, but usually quiet. Unlike tonight." He grinned and took the gun from his back pocket and placed it into a satchel on one of the stools. He picked up his phone from the kitchen bar, its screen illuminated with the scantily-dressed image of a young woman's Tinder profile. "Besides, I can't bring a girl like this meet with Mom. Can I?"

Nate remembered Patrick's mother. A plump, vibrant woman, whose curly thick hair her son inherited, was the company's CEO after her husband... no, her ex-husband. He was killed in a bar fight, as Nate recalled from the office chatter. Some thought it funny that the company's Chief

Operations Officer, Patrick, still lived with his mother. Nate never did and felt annoyance at his coworkers' privileged gossip. He still lived with his father and aunt.

"I remember Lois. How is she doing?" As Nate asked, a tinge of doubt crossed his mind, as if Patrick would tell him she had died.

"Oh you know. A bit ornery, but doing good. She's a bit put out that I moved back in with her after I needed some space from my girlfriend." Patrick swiped the image on Tinder and turned off his phone's screen.

Nate felt his face flush. "Hey, man, I didn't mean to interrupt whatever you were up to…"

Patrick shook his head. "No problem, dude. I was mostly just bored." He put the phone in his back pocket and went to the kitchen. "Let me see if I can find something for your hands."

As Patrick began riffling through the kitchen cabinets, a sensation that something was wrong agitated Nate's mind. No, not wrong, exactly. Just different. As Patrick looked under the sink, Nate realized his hands were smooth. His neck, too. Nate remembered scars creeping up his neck, to the jawline. And his left hand withered and almost useless. But both hands were whole. The memory—for it felt like a recollection more than a dream—came from the same murk as the nickname.

Patrick closed the kitchen cabinet and, seeing Nate staring at him, cricked his neck. "Well, I don't have much first aid here, but maybe I can find something to help in there." He motioned to the pantry door Nate was leaning against. Nate stepped aside, and Patrick opened the door. "Tell me how you ended up here, if that's okay?"

Nate leaned against the counter, unsure how to begin. He ended up on the streets after Patrick fired him, but he didn't want to lay that trip on the man. After all, Patrick gave Nate more opportunities than he deserved to stay on the payroll. He knew Nate had talent as a programmer, giving him a break on deadlines for the accounting systems' overhaul he tasked Nate to complete. The condition was that Nate was to attend AA meetings, but when he found out Nate had been forging his attendance records there, he had no choice but to let him go.

Nate sighed. "I screwed up. Again. Got in a fight with my dad." No, that wasn't entirely right. He looked down, fighting back tears. "And my aunt. She threw me out of the house."

Patrick nodded while riffling through the pantry shelves. "Rough deal, man. How long ago was that?"

"Almost two years."

Patrick whistled and turned to Nate, a pair of yellow kitchen gloves in his hands. "Long time to be on the streets."

"Well, I crashed with friends for a while." Friends he met at bars. Friends he stole money from. Friends he lost. "Then I tried shelters." His drunken and drugged rages got him thrown out of those quickly enough. "They were too restrictive. Been on the streets for, maybe, the past year." Since he last tried to return home. When Aunt Peggy wouldn't let him past the driveway.

Patrick walked to the studio's closet and pulled out a blue bathrobe. "Use the shower. I just had the place serviced, so everything's clean." He placed the robe on a hook inside the bathroom door and then put the kitchen gloves on the sink. "The water will probably hurt those hands, so use the gloves. I'll head out and get some first aid."

"This is all really nice of you."

Patrick shrugged. "No problem." He walked to the front door and then turned to Nate. "Well, my girl and I were supposed to be in the Bahamas this week, but after our fight, she went with a girlfriend instead. Maybe this good deed will get me some better karma." He paused, his eyes looking upward as he searched his thoughts. He opened his mouth to say something but then stopped. A moment later, he said, "Besides, I remember you as a good man, maybe you just need a break."

Nate wore the rubber kitchen gloves as he showered. Patrick was right, the blisters on his hands were too painful to run under the water and hold the soap without some sort of protection. Brown layers of dirt swirled down the drain as he washed. He soaped his hair and beard, the grit of the weeks since his last shower falling around his feet and disappearing down the drain. The warm water felt soothing, but his legs shook along with his hands as his stomach seemed to coil and churn. He needed food. No, he needed food and a fix. Especially a fix. He'd be heading to the DTs if he didn't get something soon.

He finished the shower, feeling a flash of shame at the dirt that settled in the basin. The shower head was on a hose, so he pulled it down and rinsed the tub. He dried off and then went to the sink. Patrick had left him a fresh razor to shave with, so he lathered up shaving cream and spread it over his thick beard. He wished he had scissors to clip it first, but the fresh blade was sharp enough he could shorten the beard first with the safety razor and then shave off the rest with a fresh application of cream.

When he was finished, he looked at his cleaned face in the mirror. His hair was long. He couldn't remember the last time he had it clipped. He leaned in, noticing crow's-feet around his eyes and flecks of gray in his light brown hair. *Gray and wrinkled at twenty-something...* He paused and thought. Two years, more or less, on the streets. *Twenty-six. Might as well be forty. Shit, the street aged you, bubba.*

Something else in his face, though, chilled him. An even older version of this face, looking back at him. Yelling at him. A distant memory, perhaps a fight he had with Dad although his father never invoked the distress Nate felt at the visage. It felt more like an almost-forgotten dream.

Nate shook his head to clear the thought and then carefully removed the rubber gloves, which stuck to the oozing blisters on his fingers. He then carefully put on the bathrobe. Patrick had taken his clothes to the laundry room to wash while he was out.

He opened the door but stayed in the bathroom, sitting on the toilet lid. The empty apartment still gave him a tremor of dread, and he was too agitated from hunger and detox to try sleeping. Staring at the apartment's walls would only increase his anxiety. *Something bad had happened here.*

Nate sniffed at the thought. *So, now I'm psychic?*

Still, an image of a young woman's pale face, her eyes wide with shock and disbelief, sent a deep sadness through him. Not fear or shock, just sadness. God, he needed a drink.

Nate stood up and paced the room. He'd go outside, but didn't feel comfortable dressed only in a bathrobe. He sat on the bed and examined his feet. They had been bothering him all night, but compared to his hands, the pain was negligible. He'd been walking around without socks for ages, so the blisters on his heals and toes didn't surprise him. The cuts around his soles, however, reminded him of running barefoot through glass and rock, someone pursuing him. They were healing, but he couldn't remember exactly when they happened. Another certainty fell over him. It happened somewhere around this apartment. But how could that be?

Nate flinched at the sound of keys in the lock. A voice sounded in his head, a young woman, angry and disappointed, *Nate! Open the door. Nate!*

Nate shuddered at the silent cry in his mind. It felt real, and close, with shame falling over him, along with the sense of horror yet to arrive.

The door swung open, and Patrick stepped inside holding a couple of plastic grocery bags.

Nate stood up, the turmoil inside clawing its way

out of him with rage. "Where the fuck have you been? I'm going fucking crazy here!"

Patrick stopped, his face paling. "I got you some things, man."

"Aw, shit." Nate turned and paced to the bathroom and then back, his face reddening. "I'm nuts, man. Don't you know that? Why did you let me stay here?"

Patrick closed the front door with his foot and put the bags in the kitchen. "You need food. And this." He pulled out a flask of bourbon and handed it to Nate.

Nate stepped over and took it from Patrick, pulling open the cap and gulping some down. It burned in his throat and stung as it flowed down to his empty stomach, but a warmth enveloped in his chest and head. He gulped down more, emptying the twelve ounce bottle.

He floated in a blessed detachment from the room around him as he sat down on the edge of the bed. "Sorry," he said.

"Here." Patrick pulled the wrapping off a ham and cheese sandwich and handed it to Nate. He took it and ate, gulping the sandwich down as quickly as he did the flask.

"Careful, buddy," Patrick said. "Don't get yourself sick."

"Okay," Nate said, wrapping his arms around himself. He leaned forward and back, the nausea that had been growing in him soon subsiding. As his stomach settled, a heavy exhaustion poured over him. "Oh, god, I'm tired."

Patrick sat next to him, a bundle of gauze and a jar of ointment in his hands. "Sure, you can sleep, but first let's take care of those hands. Okay?"

Nate spread the ointment on his hands, a cool balm that helped numb the itching sting. Patrick helped him wrap the gauze around his hands and then secured it with metal clips that came with the package.

"There, buddy. Now you can sleep."

Nate nodded, unable to speak or he would embarrass himself by blubbering. Patrick was being so *nice* to him. It had been a long time since anyone did anything nice for him.

As Nate pulled himself into the bedcovers, Patrick stood up and went back to the kitchen. "I'll be back in the morning," he said. "If you need anything before then, use this." He set a cell phone on the small table next to the bed. "I programmed my number into it."

Nate nodded, and he was asleep before Patrick turned out the lights and left.

20

He slept deep and dreamless but for occasional figments that flashed hot before him. A gun firing in his hand. A burning house. A young boy's face. He rolled under the covers, flat on his stomach, to quell a scalding nausea. He woke once, glancing at the time displayed on the cell phone's screen: 3:11. A fresh flask of bourbon sat behind it on the table. Nate drank down half of it. Numbed, he drifted back to sleep.

At one point, he heard sounds in the room. Soft footsteps on the carpet around the bed. He flickered his eyes, but the light in the room hurt his head and exhaustion overtook his curiosity regarding the visitor. He hadn't slept in a bed in months, and he felt as if he were floating on a cloud. He drifted back into slumber.

Hours later, he woke once more and, relieved he hadn't pissed himself, staggered to the toilet. When he finished, his head throbbed and hunger churned in his gut. He shivered and pulled the bathrobe tighter around him. His bandaged hands itched and throbbed. Walking back to the main room, he saw on the kitchen counter a Styrofoam container. Inside were sausage and eggs. Using the exposed tips of his fingers, he clawed at the food and wolfed it down, not bothering with the plastic ware that had been set next to the container. A thick paper cup contained coffee, which was lukewarm but fine for washing down the breakfast. Under the coffee cup, he discovered a folded piece of paper. In it was a handwritten note, but he couldn't get his eyes to focus and put it aside.

Nate returned to the bed. On the small table, he found an open bottle of aspirin. He spilled some out on the tabletop and picked up four with his fingertips, putting them in his mouth. With the remaining bourbon, he drank them down. Glancing at the cell phone, he saw it was after ten in the morning.

He couldn't remember the last time he had so long an uninterrupted sleep. Crawling under the covers once again, the pain in his head and hands felt distant, if still annoying. But his belly was satisfied, so he shut his eyes and fell back into a restless sleep.

He dreamed of Aunt Peggy. He knocked on her bedroom door. When she opened it, a smile formed on her haggard face, deepening the dark lines under her eyes. She hugged him as if she hadn't seen him in years, and his chest swelled with a deep lament, a yearning to never release from her firm embrace.

When Nate sputtered awake, he was certain she had died. It felt more a memory than a dream, like he had gone to his father's house to visit her at the request of someone. A young, distressed woman with blond highlights and light brown eyes. *Cheryl.* Nate shook his head. Impossible.

Yet the sense that Peggy was dead came to him with a ferocious certainty. Months earlier, Nate saw his father downtown, looking among the tents and hovelled corners of the homeless men and women, and Nate was certain he was looking for him. Nate evaded him that day, and he didn't return, to Nate's relief. Now, sitting up in the bed, he wondered. Was Dad looking to tell him something had happened to Peggy? Was he seeking Nate out to invite him back home?

Nate glanced at the time. It was after five in the evening. He had slept the entire day. He got up and walked to the kitchen, opening mostly empty cabinets, looking for any stash of alcohol that Rico... *Patrick*... might have left him. His hands trembled, the skin underneath the bandage rising to a ferocious itching that bordered on unbearable pain.

He grabbed the aspirin bottle and took four more, downing them with water from the sink. Then he checked the handwritten note. His eyes were clearer now, and he could read the message left for him: *Be back at six with dinner and to help you with bandages. Fresh clothes by the bed. Patrick.*

From where he stood, Nate could see a pile of folded clothes at the foot of the bed. One set was his old clothes, but the other was new, still with tags. He pulled off the tags with his teeth and dressed in the new jeans and pullover shirt. It was chilly in the room, so he pulled on the long-sleeved sweater, struggling against his bandaged hands to get them through the arms.

He sat on the bed and, despite his tremors and the hunger picking away in his gut, he tried to find something to read on the smart phone. It was a basic model but apparently had a data connection so he could browse for news. His head, however, hurt looking at the bright screen, so he put the phone down.

His boredom soon grew to frustration followed by resentment. *Who is he, anyway?* Nate thought. *Making me some sort of charity project?* He would be indebted to him. *Probably exactly what he wants.* Just like the day he fired Nate, complete with crocodile tears, telling him, "I hate doing this… I gave you every opportunity… I can no longer ignore…"

Become dependent on someone, and the next thing you know, they abandon you, force you out. Just like Dad. Just like Peggy. And they make you feel bad about it, too. Like that night, Aunt Peggy stood in the driveway in her quilted bathrobe, not letting him into the house, sending him away.

Aunt Peggy. It hit him again. *She died. I know she died.*

By the time Patrick arrived, Nate had dried his eyes and blown his nose, but a sharp pain stuck through his temple like a dagger. The pain subsided a bit at the sight of a bag of takeout from a nearby Mexican grill. Patrick also had a bag of things from the grocery store.

"Here," Patrick said, putting the bags on the

kitchen counter. "Change the bandages, and then we'll eat."

"I'm starved, man." Nate grabbed the bag of Mexican food and looked inside. "Let me eat first."

"I couldn't make it at lunchtime," Patrick said as they ate beef burritos and chips, sitting on stools at the counter. "But when I came in the morning you were dead to the world, so I didn't know if you'd get your breakfast around lunchtime anyway."

Nate shrugged but felt a twinge of resentment as he finished his burrito. He shook his empty Coke cup. "Got anything stronger? I'm getting the shakes."

Patrick put down his burrito and fished in the grocery bag, pulling out another bourbon. "Eventually, you'll need a better treatment than just feeding your dependency."

"Great, thanks for the tip. Never would have thought of that." Nate cracked open the lid and took a swig. The smoky bite felt good going down his throat, warming his chest and head.

"I printed up some local programs I found online." Patrick pulled a folded sheet of paper and put it on the counter.

"Gee, wow." He resisted the urge to throw the bottle at the man and finished the bourbon, the liquid's numbing blanket dampened on a full stomach. "If I didn't think I hit rock bottom already, this sure drives it home."

"Well, shit." Patrick threw away the remains of his burrito and crumpled the paper wrap around it. "You crawled in here out of the streets…"

Nate slammed the bottle onto the counter. "I can't figure out why you're helping me."

Patrick sighed and pointed at him. "Because those hands could get infected?" He pulled out fresh bandages from a grocery bag and handed them to Nate. "If you don't change the bandages soon, you might need an ER after all."

Nate sat on the bed to remove the bandages while Patrick cleaned up the kitchen. The cotton gauze pulled at his skin as he took it off, the dried ooze from the blisters feeling like he was removing skin. He tried not to flinch or show his discomfort to Patrick, or he might come over to help. Once he finished, he spread on fresh ointment and put the fresh gauze on, this time not as thickly layered, so he could still use his hands. As he worked, his thoughts strayed to when he was young, Aunt Peggy putting a bandage on his scraped hand. *The boo-boo is all fixed now. Right Nate?* The memory stung as he remembered his recent dreams.

Patrick waited until Nate finished and then said, "Well, at the risk of offending you, I can let you stay here for a while. Or if you want, I can take you back to whatever alleyway you came from."

He knew Patrick was trying to help, but he had tried to help Nate once before. Would his performance review fare any better this time?

Nate fought the temptation to bask another night in the soft bed. Biting into his inner cheek, he shook his head. "Actually, I'd like it if you took me to my father's house."

21

As the orange-tinged cobalt of twilight faded to the pure pitch of night, Nate directed Patrick out of the downtown area, leading them to the older suburbs of West Central.

Nate looked out the windshield, trepidation humming through his body. "Look for Autumn Lane. It's just a few blocks down, Rico." He looked over at Patrick, catching himself. "Patrick, I mean."

"I'll tell you something," Patrick said, slowing to read the street names. "When you worked for us, you reminded me of a man who was once really nice to me. The weirdest thing, though, is that he called me Rico, too."

Nate shrugged. "Well, Pat-Rick. Rico. Makes sense."

Patrick hit the brakes. "Holy shit, that is *exactly* what he told me, too." He stared at Nate.

Nate looked at Patrick's face. An uncomfortable image of a little boy in a cowboy costume flashed in his mind. He shifted his gaze out the windshield. "I don't know what to tell you, man. Maybe we met before you hired me way back when."

Patrick turned and moved the car forward. "No, I was just five."

The conversation added to the edge Nate already felt, so he pointed out the windshield to change the subject. "It's coming up, Autumn Lane."

Two streets down, Patrick turned left into the neighborhood. As they drove down the neck toward the horseshoe of the cul-de-sac, Patrick slowed down, his eyes taking in the old neighborhood. "I swear I've been here before."

"The house is here." Nate pointed at the dark house sitting at the mouth of the cul-de-sac's loop. Illuminated by the streetlight across from it, the window shades were drawn and the porch light unlit.

Patrick pulled the car into the driveway and shifted the car into neutral. "I'll wait to be sure you get inside."

Without a word, Nate got out of the car. Aunt Peggy always turned the porch light on after dark until bedtime. The last time he was here almost a year ago, Peggy confronted him in the driveway, clutching her quilted bathrobe against the chill wind.

"You can't come in," she had told him, explaining his father was making progress, and Nate's behavior would only set him back.

Nate had heard the words, but all he could focus on was the pattern of cartoon rabbits on her robe. *She's dressed in fucking white bunnies while throwing me to the four winds.*

He protested in anger (*It's my home!*) and then promised to stay sober (*I'll do anything you ask!*). Then he begged to come back home (*Please, I have nowhere else to go.*). She had heard it all before and shook her head, telling him to leave, her face gaunt and exhausted. She told him to get help, to get back on his feet, but he had to do it on his own this time. She had paid for his earlier rehab with funds from her investment accounts, but he always quit and soon fell off the wagon. She didn't even bother offering this time. She just sent him away.

The memory tightened the apprehension he already felt as he approached the front door that shone brightly in Patrick's headlights. *She won't be here.* Of that thought, he felt certain. He had no more chances of making amends to the aunt who raised him. Now standing before the house, a foreboding rose within him that his earlier premonition was true, that she had died. Not just that, but she had died after days of acting strange, starving herself to the point of a stroke. He didn't know how he could know this, but the idea clawed at him and would not let go.

He rang the doorbell and heard the chime deep inside the house, so at least the power was on. Maybe his father was in his bedroom at the back of the house. Maybe even Peggy would answer, putting to rest all his strange thoughts.

"Dad! Open up!" He pounded on the side of the security screen, the metal door rattling. The raw burns on his hand flared with pain and he pulled it back, hugging his fist to his chest. He rang the bell again.

The engine to the car sputtered to silence and Patrick got out, keeping the headlights turned on. "Could there be a spare key hidden around here somewhere?"

"There used to be one buried under those rocks." Nate motioned toward the corner of the garage entrance. "But I'd bet not anymore." Peggy would have made sure it was removed, so Nate couldn't use it after she forced him out. He shivered as a cold wind picked up. "Maybe we should go."

Patrick shook his head. "Let me check first." He

walked over to the bed of river rocks and started pulling some away, digging a little in the dirt.

Nate pressed the doorbell again and again, hoping to annoy his father enough he would open up the door, even if just to send him away again. He glanced toward Patrick when his eyes caught sight of a man crossing over from the house across the street.

"Heads up," he called out to Patrick.

Patrick saw the man and stood up, brushing dirt from his hands on his dark blue Dockers. As the man entered the driveway, Nate recognized him as Robert, one of the two middle-aged men who had moved into the house across the street about ten years earlier.

"Hey, Robert," Nate said, forcing a smile and raising one bandaged hand in greeting.

"Nate Johnson?" The man extended his hand but saw Nate's bandages and put it down. "Everything okay?"

"I just thought I'd visit the family with my buddy." Nate hoped he looked nonchalant and that the neighbor hadn't already called the cops. Did Robert even know he had been thrown out? Nate didn't know how close Peggy and his father were with the neighbors although he remembered Peggy had gone to the two men's wedding a few years earlier.

Robert's shoulder slumped. "You don't know?"

The ground seemed to drop out from under Nate as certainty settled in that the neighbor was about to confirm his premonition. He staggered back, pressing against the front door to steady himself. "My aunt?"

"I'm so sorry. It happened about three months ago. The paramedics came, but she had already passed. Your father took it really hard."

Patrick moved to stand by Nate and placed a hand on his shoulder. "Lean forward and breathe, buddy."

Nate leaned over, the fingers of his bandaged hands pressing on his knees, and heaved in air. "I need to see my dad."

"We were trying to find a key," Patrick said to Robert, "because he wasn't answering."

Robert took a deep breath. "Well, we haven't seen him in almost two months. No one on the block has. Some saw him drive off with a bunch of boxes packed into that old Cadillac of his."

Nate's ears buzzed, his heart thumping. Somehow, the confirmation of Peggy's demise triggered a path to memories that opened like wounds bleeding into his head. He pushed them back before they could take hold, but a resigned understanding settled over him. God, he needed a drink. He needed to fall flat on his back in a wasted blackout and hope never to wake again.

After Nate calmed, Robert offered his spare key. Peggy had provided him one after Dan locked himself out while she was away. As Robert crossed the street to get it from his house, Nate looked on. Robert's house didn't exist before. It had been a different house.

No, that wasn't right. That other house burned down. He remembered as a child the excitement of all the fire engines and smoldering wreckage.

Yet it never burned down. Someone else lived there. A friend.

Nate looked over at Patrick, who stayed close in case Nate's distress caused any further physical imbalance. Patrick gave him a reassuring smile. *Of course*, Nate thought. *Rico*.

He looked over at Robert's home. The original house in that lot *did* burn down, he was certain. He had seen the fire, not only as a child, but just a day ago, from the home's backyard. After *he* had started it. The irreconcilable memories dueled in his head, yet both were true.

Nate looked down at his hands. *So, that's how I burned them.*

22

Once inside the house, Robert, to Nate's relief, headed back to his place without going inside, but Patrick followed Nate into the living room. He wanted to be left alone but decided it wasn't a bad idea to have someone else around for a few minutes as he checked out the house.

The room was dark, but Nate flicked on the switch to the ceiling light by the door. Nate inhaled the chill, stale air and moved to open the front window for circulation. He flicked the latch but couldn't pull up the large sash with his injured hands. Patrick walked over and did it for him.

Nate walked to the family room and kitchen, turning on lights and snorting sharply at the sting of a foul odor, probably spoiled food in the refrigerator. Unwashed dishes also lay in the sink, crawling with drain flies and large roaches.

"Shit, Dad left a mess," he said to Patrick.

Patrick helped Nate, grabbing a couple of garbage bags and emptying the refrigerator. Patrick did most of the work because of Nate's hands. He emptied the sink, Nate telling him not to bother even washing the dishes, just to get rid of them.

While Patrick worked, Nate checked the other rooms. He paused at the open door to Peggy's bedroom. The closet was empty, her desk cleared, the bed an empty mattress stripped of any sheets. He imagined his father emptying the room and then realized it wasn't just imagining but a memory, watching Dad erasing Peggy from his life. Yet that couldn't have happened. Except it did. In some other life.

He didn't look into his own old bedroom, afraid his father had emptied the room long ago, and seeing it barren felt too much to bear. He instead looked in his father's bedroom, finding it mostly as he remembered.

The room across from his father's was closed, the media room his father was always showing off. Nate turned the knob, but let it go, unopened. He didn't like the sensation that ran through him, like he was invading someone else's space. Not Dad's, but someone else's.

Fearing the memory, Nate pushed it away. He wanted a drink, so he returned to the kitchen, where he hoped to find something left in the pantry. Before he could check it, Patrick walked in the back door after placing the garbage on the back porch and then started washing his hands in the cleaned sink.

"Is there anything else that needs to be done?" He dried his hands on a white towel and hung it on the refrigerator handle.

"Thanks, I got it." Nate didn't want to drink in front of him again. He didn't want to share anything he found in the pantry, either.

Patrick eyed him. "It might not be a good idea to be alone…"

"I'm not going to do anything stupid," Nate interrupted. Patrick looked hurt, and Nate added, "I appreciate what you've done, but I'd like to have some time alone to sort all this out, you know."

Patrick looked at him and then nodded. "Okay. You still have the phone I loaned you? I'll call you in the morning."

Nate patted the phone in his front pocket. "Sure." He walked Patrick to the front door and watched from the front window until Patrick backed the car out of the driveway and headed up Autumn Lane.

The first thing Nate did was check the pantry. To his frustration, the shelves were mostly empty, and none contained any of his father's usual variety of booze. Nate imagined Peggy wouldn't have tolerated any in the house, but he had hoped Dad restocked after...

Nate cut off the thought, ashamed of his anger toward his father for not stocking back up after Peggy wasn't around any longer to harangue him about drinking. Shit, for all he knew, Dad might have gotten sober for good.

Not likely. If Nate knew his father at all, he knew his father would have kept a secret stash somewhere in the house. Nate remembered one spot and headed to the master bedroom.

His father kept a metal file cabinet next to a makeshift desk built from the vanity Nate's mother had used. It had four drawers, and Nate pulled open the third one down. It in were papers related to his mother.

When he was a teenager, he had snooped through the files, trying to learn more about the mother he'd barely known and Dad avoided talking about. Even Aunt Peggy was reluctant to speak too much of her sister. He was only four when she died, and Nate had wanted to know what she was like as well as the details around her death, which he knew only had involved a car accident.

He found a file marked "Katherine C. Johnson, nee Mayfield," and in it he found a copy of his parents' marriage certificate, her birth certificate, and a blue and white certificate of death. Included among this was a coroner's report describing the conclusion she had fallen asleep at the wheel. That part upset Nate, for he remembered she had been up all the night before taking care of him while he had a high fever. If he hadn't been sick, she wouldn't have been sleepy driving in to work. She would still be alive.

The next detail on the report, however, seemed even worse for fourteen-year-old Nate. At the time of her death, his mother had been eighteen weeks pregnant. A girl.

If not for keeping his mother awake that night, not only would she have lived, but Nate would have had a baby sister. A sister he knew would have been named Cheryl, after a grandmother who died before he was born.

Behind this line of files, Nate had found a paper bag stuffed into the back of the drawer. Inside, it contained a plastic pint of Skol Vodka. Fourteen-year-old Nate had his first taste of liquor that day.

He had his first taste of how it could quell his darker thoughts and ease his grief.

Now, in this empty house, his aunt dead, his father god-knows-where, Nate found what he sought nestled in the back of that same file drawer. It was full, so perhaps Dad bought it ages ago and forgot about it. All the better for Nate.

He grabbed the bottle and cracked it open.

It took Nate the full bottle before he worked up the nerve to go into the room across from his father's. He turned the knob and opened the door, flicking on the light.

The room had changed little since he last saw it. On the wall hung an eighty-inch LCD television. On the opposite wall, a three-seat sofa and two small lounge chairs sat with small end tables between them, and a narrow coffee table in front of the sofa. Dad's media room, where he and his father watched endless hours of movies and television while Nate grew up, and then father-and-son drinking when Nate was old enough.

Those memories, however, paralleled another set, ones where this room had a poster of some guy in a bubble-gum-colored shirt named Harry Styles, and a print of Dali's *Persistence of Memory*, redone with tabby cats. A white desk had sat under the window where a girl had studied, her back to the door, so Nate could sneak up and frighten her. A girl who grew to be a young woman in this room. To whom Aunt Peggy was like a mother. A young woman named Cheryl. Recollections from that same road of memories as that nickname for Patrick he couldn't stop saying. *Rico.*

Nate opened the closet of the room, which had been converted to a pantry with snack foods and, at one time, rows of gin, vodka, tequila, bourbon, whiskey and all assortments of mixers. His father's private bar.

Most of the shelves were empty but for one with assorted boxes of crackers and snack candy. Nate ran his hands over a plastic jar of colorful M&M candies.

M&M Day. The phrase echoed with the melancholy of a sad dream. Nate pushed the candy jar aside.

Behind the M&M's and cracker boxes, Nate found three bottles of liquor, each a fifth, two of them vodka, and the other gin. So, Dad *had* done some restocking and, even in the house alone, felt the need to hide them. Nate grabbed one of the vodka.

Nate crashed on the couch and drank. He had erased Cheryl from existence. He had burned down the house the McVeys would move into, preventing his mother from carpooling with Lois McVey, which led to her having to drive herself to work after an exhausting night caring for his fever. He killed her years before she died in his other life, this time taking his unborn sister with her.

Nate entered the hallway and stood before the closed door to his old bedroom. He knew it would be empty, stripped of everything that showed Nate once existed in this house. Dad would have done that, just like he did with Peggy. Best to find out now and get it over with.

Nate swung open the door and flicked on the light.

Inside, his old bed lay under the back window, his desk sitting by the wall where it had always been, a chair neatly tucked underneath. A bookshelf stood alongside the desk, his book collection neatly stacked along its six shelves. His closet still had his clothes.

Nate stepped inside, his chin quivering. Dad didn't erase him. Dad had kept everything in its place. The room even looked like it had been dusted, his desk and books as clean as could be expected in a place vacant of life for two months. Considering what Dad had done to Peggy's room, he didn't harbor hard feelings toward Nate. His father had hoped Nate would one day come home. He even came looking for him that time downtown, when Nate, in his shame, avoided him. Now he was gone, and Nate had no idea where to even start looking for him.

Nate sat on his bed, placing the vodka bottle next to him. Something flat and black protruded from under the pillow. Nate pulled the object out. A black, leather-bound notebook. Before he even opened its cover, he knew what the first page would read: *The Journal of Margaret Lynn Mayfield.*

23

Nate flipped through the pages of his aunt's journal. The text looked familiar, as did the sudden change from her neatly scripted recipes and recounting of day-to-day events into rows of haphazardly printed parenthetical numbers and letters. After pages of this data, her writing transitioned into a long-form narrative.

I awoke today in utter confusion. I succeeded, oh god, yes, I succeeded, but at what? I fixed one thing and broke so many more. What have I done?

Nate scanned the first paragraphs, an agony of laments, and then a sentence chilled him with its familiarity: *Katherine wouldn't speak to me after Nate died.*

He read the following pages, the text flowing past his eyes as it explained a narrative of a terrible car accident and fire. He could only skim past the words as a thrum of panic spread from his gut to his chest.

Nate put the journal down and grabbed the vodka, taking a deep swig from the bottle. *This is fucking crazy.* The spirits burned down his throat, and the tension eased.

He picked up the journal again, reading through his aunt's unending guilt over his death and her discovery of a way to repair the damage, a method of returning to that terrible moment in the past and rescuing the nephew who should never have died. The tale felt familiar, as if he had read this before, a long time ago. He skimmed through the pages until he reached a section of his aunt's narrative he didn't recognize.

The Journal of Margaret Lynn Mayfield

That night, I took the jabberwock to Centennial Park South and sat on a bench near the fountain with a sculpted sundial. Despite the forest green running suit I wore, I shivered in the night air. From here, I would have a view of the accident, a moment I dreaded to witness, but this was the only way I could take the actions that would repair the broken lives my cowardice wrought. I had practiced this process several times, and the effect would happen within moments, as long as I concentrated on where I intended to go. No, not where, *but* when.

I turned on the jabberwock, the music-box chimes sounding in the cool night air. The lights flashed, and I looked into them. Cars passed on the highway that cut through the park, and anyone spotting me would probably think I was a nutcase. It didn't matter. I focused on the lights and music, concentrating on that wretched morning and ignoring the fears of what I would see and the dangers inherent in my task. For months, I had trained my mind for this moment.

The chords hit, and I felt that familiar, warm chill move under my skin. The music continued, and the colored lights disengaged from the jabberwock, circling my body like fireflies. Darkness formed around me and I floated with the lights, letting them carry me to my destination.

As I had already noted from my many test runs, I experienced the sensation of waking up. Had I not practiced this temporal travel before, I might have thought I'd slept the night on the bench. A group of children played near the sundial fountain, splashing water at one another in the bright morning sunlight. Overhead, white clouds dotted the blue sky as birds chirped in the trees. As expected, my jabberwock was nowhere to be seen. It would return to my arms when I returned.

I knew by the sun's position that it was morning, but

the exact time I could not tell. I stood up and approached the fountain. The spire in the center sprayed water, and its shadow stretched across the waters to Roman numerals etched into the pool's basin. From the etched fifteen-minute increments between each numeral, I determined it was nearly eight thirty. I had just five minutes before I would need to take action, assuming I had arrived on the correct day. My practice had been successful before, so I felt a cautious optimism that I had arrived at the point in time I had intended. Unlike my earlier trials, instead of hours or days in the past, I should have arrived eighteen years earlier, but I wouldn't know for certain until I witnessed what I dreaded to see.

I paced with nervousness for that moment to arrive, trying to remain focused on what I needed to do to accomplish my task. And then the moment arrived.

I cannot bring myself to write about what I witnessed, only that it was far worse than I could ever prepare myself. How any of us survived the initial collision is a miracle, even with the airbags that deployed after the awful impact.

After the exclamations and gasps, a horrible silence fell among the bystanders. Even I, knowing what was about to happen, froze at the sight of it. To my shame, I stood, dumb and still, even as a few men began running into the scene. Hearing a young girl behind me crying, I finally woke to take action.

I ran to the car. Flames were already creeping to our vehicle from the tanker as more gasoline spilled from its ruptured metal. I reached the back driver-side door, its metal bulging out from the bent frame of the car and already popped partially opened. I pulled on it and it sprang wider open with a crack. Shattered glass spilled over my running shoes. I ripped through the deflated airbag material that hung like curtains so I could look inside.

I saw my younger, cowardly self fleeing through the opposite door to the north curb of the park. In the car, Lois's young son Patrick crouched on the floor. He looked up at me with pleading eyes. "Help me," he said as he pulled at something.

He was pulling at Nate. My nephew was partially underneath the driver's seat, and Patrick was trying to drag him out. I immediately crawled into the vehicle, and together, we extracted Nate. I pulled Nate into my arms. I told Patrick to get out of the car. His exit from the passenger side was blocked by flames, and he crawled forward to the front seat where his mother and Katherine were still seated, struggling to get out.

My attention fell completely to Nate. I grasped his unconscious body to my chest and backed out of the car. Gasoline sloshed around my shoes and I knew it would be mere seconds before that final, horrible explosion. I carried him across the street to the south curb of the park, and set him down on the bench next to me, his head in my lap. Glancing up, I saw Katherine being pulled from the flaming car by a group of men. Lois stood near them, already having escaped. I could not see Patrick, but I knew he would have escaped as well.

Except he didn't. I gasped in horror as I saw the boy still in the car, his exit routes blocked by flames burning around the perimeter. Others around me saw him, too, and then Lois McVey began shrieking.

The explosion nearly threw me from the bench. Heat surged past my body, and the pressure in my ears crackled with a deafening pop. I held Nate and stood up, moving us further into the park, into a grassy area, where I sat down and placed him in front of me.

Smoke swirled up from the burning car and tanker. Through the waves of heat from the flaming vehicles, I could see Lois trying to get back to the car, but my younger self held her back.

I cannot write about what I saw inside that car at that moment. The memory is still too raw. All I will write is that young Patrick did not survive.

The following seconds passed as an eternity. A surge of overwhelming emotion overtook me as I cradled my nephew, alive, in my lap. But the other boy, Patrick, had not survived when I know he had lived before. My intrusion to help him with Nate delayed his own successful exit.

But Nate was alive! As I considered how I would reconcile this, I sensed an opening of new memories flow into my mind. A lifetime with Nate growing up alongside Cheryl. Patrick would be forever remembered as the hero of this day, the boy staying behind to save Nate's life with the help of a Good Samaritan bystander, a woman whose identity no one would ever learn.

Another new memory flowed in. Katherine, my dear sister, was injured with burns she did not have in my original temporal stream. My actions had somehow changed her fate, but while she would live an altered life, she would see her son grow up to adulthood, marry, and live a successful life. Katherine and I would remain as close as ever, and my investment funds and university connections would aid in her recovery. Of these things, I could carry no regrets.

As these new memories took hold, Nate's eyes fluttered open. Across the street, I saw my younger self running toward us, her distressed face streaming with tears while paramedics tended to Katherine across the road. I ran my fingers through my nephew's hair, and he looked up at me, dazed. I smiled at him and then rushed into the crowd of bystanders before my younger self reached the spot where he lay. She cried out with deep sobs, "Oh, Nate! Oh thank God, Nate! I'm so sorry, but thank God! Oh, thank God!"

Nate moaned and leaned back on the bed, placing the journal to his side. None of this made sense. His mother died when he was four. Patrick, obviously, was alive. His aunt's story didn't connect.

He tried clearing his mind, listening to the quiet of the room. He focused on the ticking of a clock, the seconds passing nearly in sequence to his heartbeats. He lay for several minutes until a click and whirring sounded, followed by the familiar mid-hour chime of his mother's bell jar clock.

Nate opened his eyes and sat up. The clock sat on a small table next to his bed. He reached out to touch its glass dome. The face of the young woman from his restless dreams flashed in his mind. He pulled his hand back, the sight of the clock filling him with anguish.

Cheryl. Aunt Peggy had mentioned her in the journal. Hadn't she? Nate picked it up and flipped through the pages. *Nate growing up alongside Cheryl.*

Nate's heart pounded in his chest. The scene his aunt described had disturbed him so much he had read right past it, but now it blazed before his eyes in Peggy's scribbled handwriting.

He was supposed to have a sister, but something had gone wrong. Nate turned the page and read on.

I walked deep into the park, reaching a copse of cottonwood and juniper, when I felt the pulling all around me. Familiar with this sensation, I knew I would return to my own time in a few moments. My view of the park dimmed to darkness and then back to light. Day and night strobing around me, the years passing as the changes of seasons flashed before me. I hadn't experienced this sensation in my short test runs. I had traveled back almost two decades, and I witnessed it passing around me with a dizzying ferociousness. I felt the ripples of my actions altering the course of the temporal stream.

But there was something else. I sensed in my flesh changes I had wrought during this reconstruction of history. The feeling disturbed me, crawling under my skin as darkness crushed around me until a panic emerged from deep in my gut.

Then I awoke here, in my bedroom at my brother-in-law's house. The life I had in Chicago was gone. I never had Kevin build my jabberwock. I never even met Kevin. I came to live at Dan's house to help him raise Nate.

This body I now inhabit is undisciplined and fat. This body never lectured before students, this mind never performed research, these hands never wrote papers or published books. I left the university life as a teaching assistant, giving up on my doctorate after my sister's death to help raise her son. A temporary arrangement, until my mourning brother-in-law could get on his feet, but his deeper demons kept me here for the boy's sake. I owed that to Katherine.

The worst part is Cheryl. Beautiful, vibrant Cheryl. I am the only one in this world who can remember her! This grief churns in my soul, too painful to endure!

Katherine is dead. She died almost twenty-two years ago. Not in the accident at Centennial Park, but alone under different circumstances, years before the accident where I intervened. Months before Cheryl could be born.

How is this possible? The alternate memories torment me, and I cannot fathom how my actions wrought the destruction in my midst. I set out to save this family yet somehow annihilated it. However I can, I must recreate my jabberwock and travel back once more to mend the temporal threads I have snapped. I owe that to everyone whose lives I destroyed.

24

A deep grief settled over Nate. He closed the journal and set it down, unable to read any more. Near him, his mother's old clock ticked. Nate looked into the clock's face, his reflection distorted in the dome's curved glass. The clock was related, in some indirect way, to what had happened.

He reached past the clock, grabbing a framed photograph on his desk. He and Aunt Peggy standing side-by-side at a fairground, smiling at the camera with their arms around each other. It was Nate's favorite photograph of the two of them, but now it seemed empty. Something was missing. Cheryl. Nate turned the frame around and read the note he taped to the back. *To my favorite nephew. Love, Pei-Pei.*

It fell upon him with a harsh force, a realization

that his actions wrought this catastrophe. The memory of dancing before the burning house seared in his mind. He held his burned hands in front of him. "Oh, god, Pei-Pei," he whispered to the empty room. "What did I do?"

He picked up the vodka bottle from the bed. *Drink*, he thought. *Drink it all away.* His bandaged hands trembled. His tongue slid over dry and cracked lips. The clear liquid gently sloshed inside the clear glass.

He set the bottle down on his desk. It could wait. He needed to go further into that murk of memories, those he had held back since receiving confirmation of his aunt's death.

He looked at the clock, focusing on the light reflecting on the glass. Nate winced as a memory punched through. His sister Cheryl her head framed in blood. Glass from the shattered clock. A gun in his hand firing, striking her. Hovering over it all, that man. That old man with his face, haranguing him into what to do. The man. Not just a man. Himself. Older. The one who made the demands to fix their broken lives.

Nate stood up, shouting into the empty air, "Where are you?" He paced his bedroom, his voice echoing against the white walls. "Come back! Show me what to do!"

Nate sat back down on the bed, feeling stupid and defeated. The vodka bottle on his desk glistened in the lamplight like the beacon of a lighthouse. *Best to forget*, he thought, *just tune out of everything*. He leaned forward and reached for the bottle.

Nate froze as a sharp, metallic rattling thundered from the backyard. The shed. Nate pulled back his arm, a spark of understanding igniting both dread and hope. *The man is back.*

The door to the shed bulged and bent at the pounding from inside. Nate entered the yard, his shoes crunching against a crust of dead leaves as he cautiously approached the metal structure. He hesitated as he arrived within arm's reach of the combination lock, jumping back at another volley of kicks and punches inside the door.

Nate deepened his voice and shouted, "Who's there?"

The assault on the metal stopped. After a brief pause, a harsh voice replied, "Tweedledee."

Nate drew in a deep breath. It was real, truly real. The man was back. "Oh, thank god," he said. "I thought I was nuts. I've been… oh, christ, can't believe you're really here."

Silence from the shed. Nate was just about to doubt his sanity once again when he heard a graveled voice. "I'm so happy for you. Now, might you be so kind as to *unlock this fucking door?*" The metal shook with a fierce clatter.

Nate took a quick step forward and grabbed the lock, turning the dial to the numbers he remembered as the combination, praying that Dad or Peggy hadn't changed it. He pulled on the casing, and the shackle released. He removed the shackle from the locking hasp, jumping back as the doors parted with a crash.

The man shambled out, a thin scarecrow in dirty, loose jeans and a stained T-shirt. The man's hand heaved out and struck Nate in the mouth with the heel of his palm.

Nate stumbled back, stars swirling before his eyes while his arms flailed and knees buckled. He fell into the brittle husks of dead foliage carpeting the yard, breaking the fall with his hands. He sat up, tasting blood in his mouth as his tongue probed his throbbing front teeth.

"That was for Ellie!" The man lumbered toward Nate and kicked him in the side. *"That's* for once again fucking this up, Tweedle*dum!*"

Nate rolled onto his side, curling into a ball. "Please stop hurting me."

The man circled Nate. "I expected after our last rendezvous that I would wake up next to my wife, enjoying the fruits of our golden life once again. But fuck no. I wake up instead in the Heights serving time for drug trafficking." He pulled back his foot to strike again, but Nate flinched and tightened the ball of his body. The older man sighed and bent over, extending his hand to Nate.

Nate reached out a tentative hand. The sight of the man brought back the memories of their last meeting in the shed. As then, the older man's arms and neck were snaked with tattoos. Flame-like images licked up his neck to a thin and pruned face. He looked older than Nate remembered, the thin, inked flesh of his arms dangling like crepe paper.

The man clenched Nate's bandaged hand in a firm grasp and pulled him to his feet, his strength far more firm than his appearance suggested. Nate looked into the older man's face, his own reflection aged by decades. Nate tilted his head, remembering something about the man's face that was now different.

"You had scars before," Nate said.

The man rolled his eyes. "Because that accident never happened. I never went back there to help Mom and royally screw our lives up. Oh, I *remember* doing all those things because the alternate memories eventually cut through, even in the drug-addled minds of us time surfers." He stepped back, extending his arms like a showman. "Now, *this* fucked up life, dear Natey boy, is all *your* creation. One hundred fucking percent *your* fault." A coiled wire dangled from one outstretched hand. The old man's glare tightened on Nate, a grimace forming on his lips.

The old man moved like lightning. He kicked Nate in the groin. Nate grunted and leaned forward, nausea groaning from his gut. The older man lassoed the silver-gray cable around Nate's neck, tightening it until he choked. Nate tried sputtering words, but only crimson spittle sprayed out.

"I got you a new necklace, buddy boy." The man's breath stank.

Nate jerked away from the man, his hands clawing at the cable around his neck, trying to pull it off. His fingers got between the woven metal and his flesh, releasing the grip on his throat enough that he could breathe more easily while the older man pulled to tighten its grip.

"Calm down, *pendejito*. You need to relax to breathe more easily. Do what I say and you'll be fine. It's just a simple cable lock I put around you. Pretty handy in a pinch.

"Now, in my back pocket is a small jabberwock I

programmed. Even with our realities annihilated by your latest folly, I still remembered how to program the damned thing after reading the journal Peggy left me under the pillow. One thing I couldn't get out of my head was when she traveled from her therapist's office to the scene of the car accident that first time she accidentally time jumped. Remember that? Took me years to get it all figured out, but it was all there in Peggy's specifications, the whole foundation. I just had to tweak it to give it more finesse. Finally, I figured out how to get the process to take you to the exact day and time you need to be. No fucking box of candy will distract you to the nether regions of temporal space this time, boy."

The older man pulled on the cable, walking Nate back into the house. Gagging, Nate pulled at the coiled metal with his fingers as it tightened over his numbing fingertips. "Stop choking me," he sputtered.

"You'll run," the older man said, pulling Nate through the family room.

"I won't. I promise I won't." Nate could barely get the words out as his older self dragged him into his bedroom, kicking the door shut with his foot.

"I was you once. Remember? I would have run if I had come to myself." The man pushed Nate onto his bed and then sat down on the desk chair, still holding the cable and pulling it taut.

Having stopped moving, the coil around his neck loosened. "You're fucking crazy," Nate shouted between deep breaths.

"I sure am, you fucking coward," the man said, gripping the cable. "You try to keep straight at least four different lives from the messes you made!" He leaned back in the chair, the metal coil twisted around his hand. "You have it easy, buddy boy. A lost sister here, a dead aunt there. I have *decades* on you, asshole! Friends, career, family and *a wife*, all wiped clean from my life." Tears streamed down the older man's cheeks as he leaned forward and struck Nate across the face. "All those memories twist and taunt me, driving me fucking insane! So, yeah, I'm goddamned crazy, alright! You will be, too, if you don't do exactly what I say."

The old man reached into his back pocket and placed a small rectangular device about the size of a cell phone on Nate's desk. "This is the new jabberwock. A lot more convenient in size than the last one, fits easily in the hand. Not that I'm going to let you touch it." He reached at his back again and pulled a gun from his waistband. "This is a little memento from the shed, which I found in that damned candy box." He placed the gun on the desk next to the device. "Scorched candy box, by the way, because I left this in the closet when the house burned. I didn't have it on me, so it restored to its proper place red-hot in this fucked-up time stream. Luckily, it didn't ignite the shed's fumes."

Nate recognized the gun, one he had purchased years ago, that Aunt Peggy took from him when he had one of his more wild, drunken fits. He didn't know she had put it in the shed, thinking she had disposed of it completely. Nate winced as a second memory crept in, where he pulled the gun from his mother's candy box in another life, in the shed with this man.

"We've done this before," he said.

"More times than I would like to consider, buddy boy. It'll come back to you. A lot already has, obviously, but it took me weeks after waking up in my cell to remember what an asshole idiot you are for what you did and didn't do, because I remembered it as something *I* did and didn't do, when I was you." The man spat air and pulled on the cable. "Such a simple plan to screw up, but not this time."

Nate gagged, pulling at the loop around his neck, but he didn't protest. His eyes focused on the gun and the device on his desk. An image of a little boy in a cowboy costume flared in his mind, the barrel of the gun pointed at the kid's face. "Rico," he whispered.

"And *what* were you supposed to do?" The old man pulled on the cable.

"Stop doing that!" Nate jerked the cable to release the old man's grip, but he pulled it back with vicious strength, the coiled metal ripping through the bandages on Nate's hands. The pull strangled around Nate's neck, forcing him forward off the bed and to his knees. As he fell, his arm struck the glass of the bell jar clock, which fell from its table to the tiled floor, the glass shattering as the clock's inner workings clanged and jingled.

Both Nate and his older self froze, their eyes locked on the wreckage. Nate saw the young woman's face again, her eyes blankly staring at him as blood pooled around her. From the look of his older self, Nate figured he was having a similar reaction. He reached down to pick up a shard of glass.

The man saw this and yanked Nate away before picking up the gun and aiming it at him. "Don't you think to try anything foolish. I've shot men before…"

"You can't kill me, you idiot. I'm you, for chrissakes." Nate sputtered and pulled at the cable.

The man blinked and grimaced, grinding his teeth.

"I'm not a fucking idiot, *pendejito*." He put the gun behind him on the desk. "But I can still *hurt* you." He pulled at the cable, tightening it around Nate's neck.

The younger man sputtered, his eyes bulging, pressure building in his head from the constriction around his neck. His vision darkened to blackness as his consciousness faded out.

When he woke to awareness again, Nate lay on his back on the concrete floor of the shed. Something clear covered his eyes, and he reached up, feeling the thin plastic of a pair of goggles and the buds stashed in his ears.

"Don't touch that," the older man admonished him from his seat on a blue folding chair. "I still got this," and he pulled at the cable noose, not enough to choke Nate again but enough to show that he could. "Now, listen carefully. I've programmed the jabberwock to take you directly to the time and place of the car accident. You shoot Rico before he can get out of the car. Now, because you broke…"

Nate sat up on his elbows. Fire burned in his throat as he struggled to speak, his voice rasping. "I can't… it never happened…"

The older man sighed. "Bingo, bubba. You get the blue ribbon. Now, let me finish, okay? Because you broke the time stream, I had to get creative with my programming. First, you will go back to the day you let the kid go. You will arrive just in time to stop yourself from burning down the house. *That* will restore the time stream to what it was before you screwed things up. Once that happens, the jabberwock will trigger again and send you back to the time and place of the car accident. You know what you have to do then."

Nate cleared his throat and swallowed, the pain easing. "What if I don't?"

The old man shrugged. "Don't what? Stop yourself from burning the house? You'll go back to October seventeenth at Centennial Park anyway and have a lovely morning before coming back to this shit hole life. Or you could reset things to our previous miserable existence and come back to that, dead sister and all. I recall the cops were about to arrest you for murder in that scenario. So, what'll it be?"

"Negligent manslaughter," Nate said, "not murder."

The man tugged on the cable. "Are you even listening to me? Is this life what you want? To grow into me? Because that's where you are headed if you don't do this."

Nate rubbed his bruised throat. Something hung against his back from the metal noose. "What's this?" he said, pointing over his shoulder.

"The jabberwock. Now, I will need to hand you this gun to take with you. You can shoot me if you want, but I don't think you will." He pointed to himself. "You realize that this drugged-out, criminal man of seventy-two is what lies ahead for you if you don't do this."

Nate remained silent, glaring at the old man.

"I know exactly what you are thinking, Natey boy. 'Oh, no! Rico is my friend! He's a good man! Took me off the streets, fed me, helped me recover!'"

Nate blushed. Those were exactly his thoughts.

"Well, bubba, I've been through this, so I know. You're his pet project, a way for him to feel good about himself. He'll even start using Rico as his name, in honor of your supposed bond. Best of friends. He'll be there for you when you learn what happened to Dad..." The old man's voice choked, and he paused. After a moment, he leaned forward and scowled. "Then Rico will get tired of you. Too much trouble. One drunken binge too many, and he'll drop you as quickly as he fired you. 'Oh, I tried *everything*. I can't let you drag me down...' Things got a little bit difficult, a teensy bit uncomfortable, and zap, I'm on my own again." He paused, the chair creaking as he leaned back. "You'll live in this house until the bank takes it away... you'll put a mortgage on it for cash to live off, of all the stupid things. Then back to the streets, buddy boy. Do I need to go on?"

Nate shook his head, absorbing the words of his older self.

"You won't miss him," the older man said. "Not in our golden life. Not at all. You read the journal. Rico will die a hero. Maybe no one will notice he was shot. The fire pretty much gets rid of everything. The death of the kid is a small price to pay for the restored lives of everyone he destroyed..."

"Stop," Nate said. "Please, just stop."

"This is the time to do it, then." The man held the gun in his lap. "If you don't do this now, eventually it'll be too late. You know, because of that particular law of time travel. Only seventy percent of our life. I won't be able to come back to you. You'll be too old to get to the date of the car accident. You'll have to go back to your *own* younger self and convince him to..."

"Oh, shit. Just shut up, okay?" Nate leaned forward, his fingers rubbing around the plastic goggles to ease his throbbing head. The old man was right. Only one thing could end this nightmare, and only Nate could do it. He had already tried other fixes, attempting less drastic changes that all ended in disaster. He had only this one option left to set things right.

Nate looked up at his older self. "You're right." He reached his hand out for the gun. "Let's get this done."

Nate sat in the blue folding chair while his older self made an adjustment to the jabberwock hanging over Nate's back.

"You'll still be in the shed. I had to guess on the timing, but I think I got it within a few minutes of when you need to act. Better too early than too late…"

"Yep," Nate said, only half-listening as the old man rambled, his fingers fondling the barrel of the gun as he focused his mind on what needed to be done.

"So, that should do it. Hang on, I'm switching on the box."

The shed filled with glowing icons, the goggles displaying three-dimensional shapes that floated throughout the room. Nate tightened his grip on the gun's handle and then checked the magazine for the third time to ensure it was in place and fully loaded.

His older self stepped forward, also wearing goggles. He waved his hands to move icons away, clicking a folder that changed the display. A single icon floated in the middle of the room, a grandmother clock with the label, *PeiPei_20.0.1.exe*.

"This is it, Natey boy. No need to concentrate, no risk of an errant thought whisking you off course. This program knows each place to take you. First, fix your mess. Then fix *our* mess. You ready?"

Despite the chilly October air, sweat dripped from Nate's forehead. He nodded in quick jerks as his sockless feet fidgeted in his shoes. *Let's do this.*

"Great. Now, one last thing. This is important: If you see a version of me at the park, ignore him. He'll be saving Mom. You will probably see Aunt Peggy, too, running to save me… you… dead to the world in the back of the car. Don't get in her way. Just focus on your one task with Rico. Shoot the kid before he can get into the front seat and…"

"Kill the fucking kid. Got it." His hands trembled as he gripped the gun.

"Right." The old man smiled like the Cheshire Cat. "Okay, bubba, make us proud." He flicked the icon with his finger, launching the jabberwock.

25

The process began, and the familiarity of it struck Nate like a long-forgotten melody. The music of chiming tones and chords that trilled throughout his skin as lights spun in a vortex of colors that lift him in a warm embrace. Then silence.

When he opens his eyes, he is still in the shed, lying on his back. A breeze from outside rustles the metal walls. It is warm, almost hot.

Nate yawns as he comes to awareness and then winces at the pain in his mouth from being hit earlier. He shakes his head to clear his mind and wake himself up. He's back, just as he was before in that other life, before his mistaken actions scourged his reality from bad to unbearable. He sits up, his bandaged hands brushing against a pair of goggles like the ones he is wearing. Remnants of his prior visit. He pushes them aside.

Standing, he stuffs the gun in the back of his jeans waistband. He won't need it. Not yet. He waits, his moment coming soon.

A minute passes. Then two. Nate fidgets with anticipation, rocking on his heels, feeling like a snake about to strike. Another minute passes, and he feels his nervousness shift to uncertainty. Should he peek out of the shed and see what is happening? Is he where he is supposed to be? The extra pair of goggles left from his prior trip give him the certainty that he must stay put. *Patience, Natey boy, patience.*

Finally, footsteps outside. Nate stands up, assuming a two-point stance. The doors slide open.

The other man freezes, staring into his own eyes, not understanding this twist to his plans. Nate lunges at his doppelganger, smacking the young man hard in the face. His other self yelps in pain, jumping back and smashing his head against the top edge of the metal doorframe.

Nate winces at a stinging ache in the back of his own head as his other self tumbles backward, unconscious, on the ground in front of him. Nate rubs his head, feeling the grainy crust of dried blood in his hair, evidence of the new history he just wrote for himself. *He won't be getting the gasoline now,* Nate thinks as he rubs his head. *The McVey house won't burn this time.*

The world flashes. Nate stands still, his other self vanishing from the ground in front of him. The sky strobes from blue to black and every shade of gray in between. Stars circle overhead, fading away from sun and clouds, and then come back to dance again. The trees shed their leaves, the ground frothing in brown, changing to white, melting to a dark brown that quickly bursts out as a carpet of green. The years of seasons flash before Nate so fast they become a blur. He steps back into the shed, placing his hands on a shelf to keep himself steady and realizing they are no longer bandaged or blistered. He closes his eyes until the kaleidoscope of shifting images stops. He feels the history restoring, the changes he made to his life reversing and reconstituting, his own body losing the alterations brought on by a life on the streets, a life he has lived no more.

"What the…"

Nate opens his eyes at the sound of the voice. Sitting on a chair next to him is his older self… only different. Younger than the one he just left. Slightly healthier. Crouched near his feet is another version of Nate, also wearing the goggles, but his eyes are closed. In a blink, he vanishes. His older self looks up at Nate. "Where the fuck did *you* come from?"

The shed door slides open, accompanied by the chirp and crackle of a radio. Two officers pull their guns. "Freeze!" Nate stands still and raises his hands, his older self following suit from his chair. "Which one of you is Nate Johnson?"

"I am," Nate and his older self say in unison.

The officers exchange confused looks and then turn back to the two men, seriously intimidating looks on their faces. "He's got to be the younger one," one officer tells his partner.

Just as they step toward Nate, the jabberwock still hanging at his back comes to life. The non-melody of music plays in Nate's ears as the lights dance around him. He is showered in them, the tingling in his skin feeling like he is swimming in carbonated water.

The shed vanishes, Nate yanked away by the swells and ebbs of temporal streams, the current pulling him to his final destination.

The darkness dissolves to light. Nate is standing under a tree, his back leaning against the rough bark. Gold and brown leaves scatter across a grassy lawn.

He blinks, attempting to make sense of his new surroundings. Like awakening after a deep sleep, it takes a moment, but then he remembers. Centennial Park. He turns around at the sound of traffic, the highway that traverses the center of the park. Two lanes on each side, with cable median barriers dividing the two directions of traffic. From that, he knows he is in the past. The cable barriers were replaced after numerous crossover accidents, like the one he is about to witness.

Nate scans the park. He is on the north side, opposite the sundial fountain his aunt wrote about. A colorful array of blankets dot the park as scattered picnickers enjoy the cool fall weather, an unusual number of people for a weekday morning. A lot of children, however, accompanied by a few adults, indicate some sort of school field trip. Near Nate, a group of four men bounce about on a basketball court and green-painted metal garbage cans buzz with flies.

He pulls off his goggles and throws them into the garbage. He removes the cable from around his neck, pulling it over his head loop by loop to rid himself of its choking restraint. The small device containing the jabberwock program dangles from the woven metal and Nate throws them into the garbage can as well. He is where he needs to be for his last task, and the devices will vanish from this temporal sphere when he leaves. He stretches his neck, grateful to be free of them.

Nate walks closer to the road. If his older self's program worked as planned, his child self is at this moment in the back seat of a car heading westward toward doom, in a childish fight with young Rico, annoying the other boy's mother, who is driving the car, with Aunt Peggy in the back with the children and Nate's mother in the front.

Nate stands near the sidewalk bordering the park and shivers. He is underdressed for the weather, but the chill will only last a short amount of time. Scanning the other side, he sees a woman with long white hair and wearing green running sweats staring into the pool of the fountain. Aunt Peggy, her older self here to accomplish her mission. Nate's heart pounds in his chest as he anticipates the coming moments.

Another man stands at the park's edge on Nate's side, about twenty feet away, his eyes scanning the road toward a large pedestrian walkway that bridges the highway, connecting the two sides. Nate squints, making out the man's features. About his height, also with the light brown hair. The face is healthy, but the features carry weathered creases along the jowls and around the eyes.

Nate is looking at himself, perhaps fifteen or twenty years older than he is now. The old man had told him he would meet this version of himself, the one that attempts to save their mother, only to be blocked by Rico. Nate feels the gun secured in his waistband at his back and hears the old man's voice in his head. *Shoot the kid before he can get into the front seat.*

The back of his neck prickles, his breath catching. The other man is looking right at him with a quiet gaze. The man's head tilts to the side, seeing the resemblance, his mouth parting as if to speak. To Nate's consternation, the man takes a step toward him.

Boom! Both men's eyes divert westward, toward the pedestrian overpass. A large diesel truck wavers underneath it on the eastbound side, the rubber of one tire slapping against the wheel well and asphalt, the large cab lurching as the driver attempts to maintain control. The vehicle is moving too fast, tilting to one side as it reaches the median barrier. With a crunch, it smashes through to the westbound side, a few cars traveling in that direction screeching their brakes as the diesel blocks their path. The trailer holding the long, silver tank crashes on its side, skidding along the road in a shower of sparks, the tank's valves popping open. Fluid spills out in a stream, forming a spreading pool on the road.

Nate instinctively steps back from the metal carnage that stops fifty feet away. His other self does the same, and both men turn their eyes eastward, into the mid-morning sun, toward the curve in the road heading west.

Several cars coming around the curve stop, the drivers seeing the blocked road ahead. All but one. A twilight blue Lexus tears around the curve, not slowing down. Nate glimpses Lois McVey in the driver's seat, her body turned to the rear seat as she scolds the boys, unaware of what lies ahead. The car impacts the diesel's cylindrical tanker, the windows of the car bursting with white as the airbags deploy. The front of the car crushes underneath the tanker, gasoline gushing out and flowing over the car in a shower.

Nate remembers to breathe. He sucks in air, his focus on controlling his shivering hands and legs, shaking his head to release the shock at what he has just seen. Reaching to his back, he pulls out the gun just as his other self, also moving to action, heads toward the car. Nate has seconds to act.

Nate follows his other self toward the car. The back passenger-side door is open, the deflated air bags fluttering in the breeze. He can see young Rico inside struggling on the floor, his back to Nate.

No turning back now. Nate raises his pistol with both hands, aiming at his target. He pulls the trigger. The gun fires with a sharp pop.

His older self jerks back, crying out in surprise and falling to the asphalt. The older man looks up. Nate stands over him as the man whimpers, "Jesus Christ, what the fuck?" Nate fires again, striking him in the gut. The man curls up, blood streaming between his fingers as he squeals in pain.

Certain the man can't get up again, Nate throws the gun aside. In the chaos, no one has noticed his actions. He turns his attention to the road, eying the other side as bystanders rush to the edge of the park. Traffic is at a standstill as Aunt Peggy, in the green running suit, crosses over the metal barrier, heading toward the back door of the car. Nate runs in front of her, cutting off her path. His aunt's face displays confusion as she realizes he is blocking her path. She adjusts her direction, moving to go around Nate when he runs at her, his arms outstretched. Her mouth drops open as Nate rushes at her, pulling her into his grip.

Aunt Peggy hollers. "Let me go. What are you doing? What are you doing!" She pushes against Nate with a force that surprises him. Her body is thin and wiry, full of strength, not the flabby, sedentary aunt he grew up with. This is the Aunt Peggy of the Before, the aunt who lived her life in the original, unaltered time stream.

"Shh," Nate tells her, trying to get her to calm down. "Shush, it's me, Pei-Pei, it's me…" She looks into his face as he talks, her head shaking. Nate smiles at her. "Yes, Pei-Pei, it's me…"

Her eyes widen. "Nate?" Her gaze shifts to the burning car. The group of basketball players is at the car, pulling Nate's mother out. Lois McVey is tumbling out of the car from the driver's side, Rico right behind her.

Her face scrunches to horror and she screams, "*No!*" She pushes at Nate, trying to get past him and to the car, but Nate's arms grasp her in a tight embrace.

The explosion knocks both of them backward. Nate pulls his aunt back over the metal barrier, his body blocking her from the worst of the scorching air that bursts around them. The fire's heat sweeps across Nate's back as the force of the shock wave sends both of them to the ground.

Aunt Peggy shrieks in grief, but Nate holds her, whispering into her ear. "It's okay, Aunt Peggy. It's okay…"

Nate glances across the street. Lois, Rico, and the

younger Aunt Peggy are huddled together. His mother is on her knees in front of them, howling with grief toward the burning car. Nate's wounded older self writhes on the ground nearby before vanishing to a wisp of steam.

He shifts his attention back to his aunt. She looks into Nate's face, her face wet with tears. "Oh, why did you stop me, Nate? Why?"

Nate caresses his aunt's face with his hand. "Thank you, Pei-Pei. Thank you for what you did." His tears drip down his face, splashing onto her as he grips her hand. "But I've seen every way this turns out. This is for the best. For everyone."

"Oh, Nate," his aunt weeps, his mother's wails echoing from across the road. "I'll never be forgiven."

"Just *talk* to her, Pei-Pei," Nate says, remembering the young woman on her phone, smelling of cherry candy. "She'll want you to."

He pauses, a sense of lightness enveloping him, an awareness of having done, at last, the one best thing he ever did. The stillness of his younger self, embraced by flames inside the car, envelopes him. Nate looks down at his aunt with a broad smile. "You know what, Pei-Pei? I didn't even feel a thing."

Nate kisses her cheek and then dissolves into a

white vapor that rides a gust of wind, joining the smoke of the burning vehicles.

Peggy slowly stands up, her cheek still tingling from his kiss. She walks into the park, away from the flames and chaos, the shouts and murmurs of the crowd, the clamor of sirens and the smell of burning fuel and materials falling behind. She stumbles as her vision clouds from an onslaught of tears.

The world around her flashes, and Peggy understands she is returning. The sensation is calming, like a baby being rocked in its cradle, or an airborne dandelion seed drifting with the wind, as the temporal vortex returns her to the present moment from which she came.

26

She sat for a long time on the bench, stars twinkling overhead, her hands gripping the wooden case of the jabberwock. Her intellectual mind tried to grasp what had happened. Grown to his twenties, he came back to stop her.

I've seen every way this turns out. The words from her nephew echoed in her mind. It could only mean she really saved him in some other life, and he came back to make sure it never happened.

Peggy stood up from the bench with a desolate slowness. She had returned to her life with nothing changed. The jabberwock's wire whiskers brushed against her arms as she walked into the parking lot, returning to her car. In the distance, a fire blazed in one of the park's garbage cans, a group of men and women standing around it for warmth.

She watched them for a moment and then unlocked the car's trunk and pulled out her papers and journal, all the materials she had written about the jabberwock that she carried with her in case she needed to reference them for her plans. Ruffling through another file, she pulled out the Polaroids taken with Kevin's camera. All the specifications in her hands, she walked back into the park, stopping at a picnic table and setting the device down.

She opened the lid of the jabberwock, exposing its circuits and soldered wires that Kevin had so skillfully built for her. She reached in and pulled at the wires, ripping them out of their fixtures. Picking up a rock, she smashed the circuits and LED lights and then pulled out the stiff wires from the side, crumpling them before tossing them among the ruins inside the wooden container.

She closed the lid and walked to the group around the burning garbage can, throwing the box and its contents inside. The others nodded at her, probably grateful for the extra fuel. She smiled wanly, standing a few minutes among them while throwing her papers and photographs into the fire. Finally, she ripped out the pages of her journal, throwing them to the flames, along with the empty leather binder. Flames ate the papers and the wooden shell of the jabberwock, a flurry of sparks spinning into the air as the materials of her obsessive work flamed to ash.

She reached her hand to her face, touching where Nate had kissed her. *Thank you*, her nephew had said. *Thank you for what you did.* Deep among the park's dark trees, an owl hooted. *This is for the best. For everyone.*

The burning materials shifted, sending sparks flying from the metal cannister. As Peggy followed the spinning gold lights that flickered upward toward the stars, a comforting lightness came over her as if she could soar to the heavens with them. She understood in that moment that something *had* changed from her brief journey to that long-ago morning. Standing in the warming glow of the burning jabberwock, she found she could, at last, forgive herself.

The Journal of Margaret Lynn Mayfield

The day after my experience I spoke to Navenka Oyibo, and she expressed her relief that I had destroyed the jabberwock and all my specifications. She said the jabberwock offered a dangerous temptation to manipulate the trauma machine that choreographs our lives. My nephew's actions indicated that the unintended consequences of my intervention must have been very dire, indeed.

I am relieved I did it that night while the entire experience was at its most visceral, giving me the clearest erudition regarding the dangers it posed. Had I not destroyed it in those moments, could I be tempted to try once more? I push this idea aside when it arises, and over the past months, I have avoided recalling the memorized elements of the jabberwock, confident I will eventually forget them.

I spoke to Kevin, my goal to determine if my teaching assistant had made his own copies of the specifications under the pretense of begging his forgiveness for the unfortunate "accident" that befell the device he built for me. He took it in stride, telling me he would build a new one if I desired (for a similar fee). To my relief, he told me I would need to give him all the specifications again. He kept no notes of his own, and that granted me tremendous solace. Of course, I told him rebuilding the jabberwock wouldn't be necessary. I truthfully told him I got the use out of it I needed.

I took a leave of absence from the university to remain near Katherine, hoping to reconnect with my sister as well as begin documenting my experiences of the past few months where it all happened.

I rejoined my family a short time later.

After years of silence, contacting my sister filled me

with deep anxiety. I could not control if she would not forgive me, but I had to try. When I spoke to Katherine, we had a difficult conversation, full of tears, but the fact is we had a conversation.

As it turned out, she had been afraid to call me, fearing I had not forgiven her! She regretted the blame she heaped on me in those awful days after the accident, coming to realize that she had been projecting onto me her own guilt over Nate's death. She was his mother, yet in her panic during the crisis, she didn't think to tell any of the men pulling her out that her son was in the back seat.

Since that day, we met in person, and I caught up with her at the house. Dan is doing well, still doing accounting work for McVey Land and Living. Katherine told me in confidence he still struggles with occasional drinking issues, but the past year has been sober, and she occasionally attends AA meetings with him as his supporter but has made her own friends in Al-Anon.

I have been staying with my sister in the guest bedroom of her house. Cheryl and her husband were in Seattle for business, but they would come into town for the upcoming October 17 reunion, and Katherine was eager to have me join them.

We met at Luigi's Linguini (the restaurateur's clever spelling), an establishment with kitschy Italian decor that the kids loved, and has become an annual pilgrimage for the family to gather and remember Nate. I recalled the *establishment from when Nate and Cheryl were children, and the owner giving them various sweets and boxes of crayons to draw on the paper place mats.*

The owner, Luigi Duranti, seated Katherine, Dan, and me at a round table in an alcove off the main floor. Seeing the man after all these years brought to me a bittersweet nostalgia and gratitude that some things do not change. Lois McVey arrived a short time later and sat next to Katherine, with me on my sister's other side. Cheryl and Patrick arrived a few minutes later, excited and giddy, and Cheryl gave me a great hug. She has grown into a fine young woman. After we all sat down, Luigi brought a few bottles of Santa Lucia to the table.

Our meal proceeded with amiable chatter, catching up with Cheryl and Patrick, who married a year earlier after a long courtship. Growing up as neighbors, and with Nate as a common link, they have known each other their whole lives, so the match comes with little surprise. The romance, however, didn't start until Patrick returned from college and continued as Cheryl finished her own degree.

Cheryl consistently referred to her husband as Rico, so I asked where the nickname originated. Lois rolled her eyes, but the young man told me he picked it up as a child, after an adult called him that while "intervening during a rather unpleasant encounter with my father."

"Patrick is such a fine Irish name," Lois said, "but everyone at the office calls him Rico, too. I'll never call

him that." She briefly lamented her late ex-husband's poor influence that turned her son against his given name while Patrick patted her arm and rolled his eyes. Cheryl mouthed in my direction, like mother, like son.

After the meal, the mood grew somber. The plates were removed and each of us poured the sparkling water into wine glasses to celebrate the reason for our gathering. Starting with Katherine, each of us gave a brief speech in memory of Nate.

"I can still see Nathan's sapphire eyes, and he had such a sweet tooth..." Katherine tearfully said, and we all raised our glasses, murmuring in agreement.

Dan fidgeted in his seat, telling the group, "Anytime I'm tempted to be less than I am, I think of my son's smile to keep me on the straight and narrow." Again, we raised our glasses in assent.

Cheryl admitted her memories of her brother were vague, being only four when Nate left us. She remembered him as "my big brother who looked out for me, included me in games with his own friends, and always let me feel I belonged."

Patrick choked up during his toast. "The accident was the worst day of my life. I never stopped thinking if I had been a just a little stronger..." Cheryl whispered something in his ear while Lois patted him on the arm, and Patrick pulled himself together, simply stating, "To my friend, Nate."

Lois raised her glass. "I still carry the guilt of being the one behind the wheel." Katherine took her friend's hand, giving Lois a forgiving smile. *"But,"* Lois continued, *"out of what happened, I gained a larger family. I also finally got the courage to focus on what is most important, like protecting my son..."* She wept, and Patrick placed a hand on her back. *"I'm good. I'm good,"* she said, blowing her nose. *"To Nate,"* she said, raising her glass, and we all followed.

It came to my turn, and I had trouble finding the words to tell the gathered family. "He called me Pei-Pei" was what first came to mind, "his special name for me from when he was very young and couldn't quite say Peggy." I took a deep breath, thinking of my recent experience. *"I know he would have grown into a sensitive, brave, and wise young man."* It was the truth, and we all raised our glasses to celebrate that.

Dessert arrived, seven slices of tiramisu dusted with a soft veil of cocoa (the seventh slice placed between Katherine and Dan, symbolically for Nate), and our conversation returned to topics of less emotional weight. Cheryl then grabbed a large white envelope from her satchel and pulled out the contents. "These are the latest ultrasounds," she said to the group.

I didn't even know she was pregnant. "Eighteen weeks, Aunt Peggy" she said, proudly touching her belly.

Cheryl held Patrick's hand as she announced, "The baby is going to be a boy."

As the group sighed and clapped, Patrick spoke up. "And we have chosen his name." He paused, his eyes glistening. All our eyes fell on the young father-to-be. He took in a deep breath. "We are naming our son Nathan Patrick."

Tears flowed down Katherine's face as she and Lois hugged the young couple, and Dan shook Patrick's hand. I touched my cheek where Nate had kissed me. His kiss had left a mark, a reddish seal from our brief encounter, and my fingers ran over its smooth surface. He chose to remain our shared history, so the rest of us could have one at all. I picked up an ultrasound, the delicate wisps and smoky shadows rendering the forming child like a charcoal sketch. As I stared at the image, I heard Nate's voice whispering in my mind, "Thank you, Pei-Pei... this is for the best... for everyone."